Anonymous

Difficulty between Chile

on the one hand, and Peru and Bolivia on the other

Anonymous

Difficulty between Chile
on the one hand, and Peru and Bolivia on the other

ISBN/EAN: 9783337383152

Printed in Europe, USA, Canada, Australia, Japan

Cover: Foto ©Andreas Hilbeck / pixelio.de

More available books at **www.hansebooks.com**

DIFFICULTY BETWEEN

CHILE,

on the one hand, and

PERU AND BOLIVIA

on the other.

General Considerations

In Relation to the Difficulty between

CHILE, on the one hand,

and

PERU and BOLIVIA on the other.

———

It is said that the agents of Peru and Bolivia, having vainly made every effort to influence the Department of State in their favor, now propose to bring their case before Congress, in the hope that that body will cause the Government to adopt active and energetic measures, and even to declare war, if necessary, for the purpose of compelling Chile to yield to the wishes of her enemies in the adjustment of the terms of peace.

Many public, and still more private documents might be cited to show that the Peruvians and Bolivians threatened to ruin and annihilate Chile, and to blot it from the map of America. When they found that their empty boasts produced no effect, they changed their tactics and now declare themselves to be the victims of overwhelming force. They assert without a shadow of truth, that Chile at the commencement of hostilities was well armed, while *they* were in a defenseless condition, whereas the fact is that Chile at that time had but little more than two thousand men under arms, and that it was proposed to sell the two iron-clad vessels which she possessed.

Everybody knows that Chile has procured her arms since the war commenced, and that six cargoes of arms have been received by her from Europe. It is wholly and notoriously untrue that Chile purchased a single rifle or a single cannon in the anticipation of a war with the Argentine Republic.

On the other hand, Bolivia and Peru are countries accustomed to war. A state of revolution has hitherto been their normal condition, and every one of their citizens has been a soldier. Scarcely can a single Doctor be found who is not at the same time a Colonel.

Chile's alleged previous arming, therefore, and her imaginary abuse of power are simply figments invented for the purpose of concealing the faulty organization and the defective moral energy of those nations.

The appeal which it is now proposed to make to the American Congress to become the champion of these degenerate nations, which have been powerless to defend their country, when a nation with scarcely half of their population has boldly asserted its rights within their own boundaries, is a fresh humiliation, in addition to that of the defeats which they have suffered on the field of battle.

In every well ordered nation, the Executive is the one who is charged with the conduct of its diplomatic affairs, because he has full knowledge of such things, and is familiar with all the details of foreign relations; it is, therefore an inversion of the plainest governmental rules to seek to induce Congress to take the initiative in matters of this kind, and to embark in foreign adventures. What a Congress may and is under obligation to do, is to disapprove any unwise steps that may be taken by the Executive in his management of the foreign affairs of the nation over which he presides. The power possessed by this great nation is due to the very fact that it has kept its domestic interests aloof from foreign complications. Such was the policy advocated by the immortal Washington, and such has hitherto been the unvarying practice of the United States.

It was, moreover, the wish of the founder of the Republic that the federal capital should be a city of small size, in
which the officers of the Government only should reside, so
that the wire-pulling and intriguing of the persons now
known as politicians and lobbyists might be avoided.

If the time-honored traditions of the American policy
be followed, there is no ground for the slightest fear that the
project now cherished by the Peruvians and Bolivians will
be productive of any result, especially since there is not the
shadow of a reason why this great people should abandon
the glorious path which it had thus far trod.

The Monroe doctrine, which has of late been brought
so prominently into notice, and which has been so distorted
that its author would not recognize it, is very simple, and
can be comprehended by the most ordinary understanding

What the distinguished American President said, and
meant to say, by his famous doctrine " America for the
Americans," was that European powers were not to interfere in the affairs of America, as America had no intention
to interfere with those of Europe. Everybody knows that
these words of Mr. Monroe were uttered at the time when
the Holy Alliance was proposing to aid Spain in recovering
her former colonies. The view entertained by him was that
the Allied powers were not to extend their system to the
New World, and that, if this were attempted, the United
States should consider such an attempt as subversive of their
peace and security, and that consequently no effort on the
part of any European power to interfere with the nations of
the Western Hemisphere should be permitted. This view
has not the slightest connection with the present situation
of the affairs of Chile, Peru, and Bolivia.

Probably the best opinion, founded on historical precedents is, that the United States would have no just reason
to take part in American questions, which do not directly
concern them, unless one or more European powers threatened to change or belittle the Republican form of government in those countries which have adopted it.

The doctrine laid down by Mr. Monroe would be
ridiculous if it were to afford room for the inference that the

United States reserved the right of interfering in the political affairs of the various sections of this continent. Such was never the intention of President Monroe, and experience has shown that the Governments of America have correctly understood the scope of the aforesaid maxim in allowing the States of America to manage and settle their political affairs for themselves, without any interference whatever.

The South American countries of Spanish origin, although small, are as independent and as sovereign as are large countries, and it would be contrary to the principles on which the North American Union is based, if, because they are small, this powerful nation should assert the right to limit their sovereignty. No man of ordinary intelligence would dare to advocate such a course.

The legitimate influence to be exercised by the United States in the New World consists in the example afforded by their free institutions, in a respect for the rights of others, in the spirit of industry and enterprise, in the salutary principle of combination for improvement in all branches of human industry, in wise and friendly direction and counsel, and in a prudent foreign policy. To seek such influence, however, in the exercise of force, even if it be only that of moral pressure, would be absurd in the extreme, and a truly fatal error. The deplorable consequences of such a policy are so well known to the statesmen of this country, that it would be but a waste of time to point them out.

Chile thought, in 1866, that she could avail herself of the Monroe doctrine, when Spain, after proclaiming, on the Pacific coast, the principle that she had a right to reassert her sovereignty over her lost colonies, threatened to burn the flourishing city of Valparaiso. The American Squadron in those waters was stronger than ever; and yet, for certain inscrutable reasons, American influence did not cause itself to be felt in that memorable contest, and Valparaiso was laid in ashes.

Is it conceivable, in view of that fact, that the United States can now contemplate interfering in political matters in which they have had no active participation, and in which they are called to act no part save an eminently peaceful and friendly one ?

The attitude of the American Government at the conference held at Arica in October, 1880, was in harmony with the antecedents of this nation,'and with the *role* which properly belongs to it in America. Chile was, and ever will be grateful for that attitude, and with the greater reason, since, for the space of fifty years, that little Republic has sedulously followed the political and administrative example of the nation which was represented, as a common friend, at that conference. The present condition of affairs is, however, entirely different.

The United States need the frank, upright and sincere co-operation of all the American Republics, in order to realize their aims. If they provoke resistance, on the ground of their superior strength, and lose the good will of some, while they gain nothing but forgetfulness and ingratitrnde from others, they will never be able to bring about the noble harmony which is required for the proper cultivation, in the New World, of the tree of liberty and democracy.

No nation in the world, however little self-respect it may have, can quietly allow itself to be arraigned before the bar of a foreign Congress for trial. Chile has given too many evidences of courage and energy to permit anyone to believe that she would do what no other nation, jealous of its prerogatives and rights, would do.

What Chile can do, has done and will do, is to give to the world those explanations demanded by international courtesy and respect, which are contained in the diplomatic documents called memorandums, manifestoes, messages and circulars.

The object of these lines, which are of an entirely unofficial character, is to enlighten the public opinion of this nation, so friendly to Chile, to correct errors and misconceptions, which are so freely circulated, owing to the very great liberty of the press; to dispel the mystifications whereby it is sought to confound facts and things, and to free certain minds from the prejudices which they have been led to conceive.

We propose to call attention to but a few of the assertions which have been most persistently repeated by the enemies of Chile, and, in so doing, we shall be as concise as possible.

THAT CHILE CAUSED THE WAR.

This assertion is absolutely false, and, fortunately, nobody now believes it.

It would, perhaps, be as well to publish the manifesto made by Chile to those nations with which she was on terms of friendship on the eighteenth day of February, 1879, when she was obliged to declare war against Bolivia; as, however, that document is too voluminous, we prefer to copy, as an appendix to this statement, the brief manifesto which was published on the 12th of April of the same year, when war was declared against Peru. We think that document will be sufficient to demolish that false assertion, and to discredit the slander that Chile declared war with a view to despoiling her neighbors.

THAT CHILE COMMITTED ATROCITIES DURING THE WAR.

This is another invention, without any foundation whatever.

The Peruvians and Bolivians, who are people of fertile imaginations, and who have never, as is well known, been distinguished for their regard for truth, have taken this assertion as the basis of exaggerations such as were never equalled by the most extravagant rhapsodist. Paper can be made to say anything, and when the pen is guided by hatred and revenge, truth is very easily sacrificed to those base feelings.

We may assert that there was never a war more humanely conducted than that waged by the Chilians in Bolivia and Peru. The same has been said of all victorious armies, or even much more, than has been said against that of Chile. We have before us a report of the atrocities said to have been committed by the American armies during the war with Mexico, and in that with the Southern secession-ists; and if one-third of those statements were true, it would be necessary to consider the Chilians as saints.

It is not necessary to consider, in detail, the cruelties said to have been committed by the Chilians, for, should we do so, it would fill a book. Suffice it to say that, as regards the expedition commanded by General Lynch against the North of Peru, (the object of which was to secure some resources from the occupied country, as is usual in all wars,) the injuries done by that officer to those who refused to pay their military contributions have been exaggerated at least eighty per cent. The same, and even more, may be said of what took place at Moquegua.

Meantime, it is sufficient to read the decrees, proclama-tions, manifestoes and messages of the leaders, who have claimed the supreme power in Peru, in order to become convinced that they are the ones who have plundered and ruined their country. They reproach one another with doing this, and assert that the different parties in Peru have done infinitely greater damage to their country than has been done by the enemy.

On the other hand, the press of Chile and that of im-partial countries have published to the world the atrocious cruelties committed by the Bolivians and Peruvians against the Chilians. Many instances might be cited in which wounded men were murdered, but it will be sufficient to refer to the burning of houses in the town of Tarapaca, the object of which was to burn alive the wounded men who were lying there, and the soldiers who were defending them-selves in those buildings, which object was accomplished. Whenever they have been able to perpetrate such revengeful acts they have done so.

But, why stop to consider details which now belong to history, and which are the sad legacy which wars leave to mankind?

But the blots which Peru and Bolivia will never be able to efface, consist, in the use of explosive projectiles, which has been ascertained beyond a doubt by the Chilian surgeons, in the expulsion of all Chilian citizens residing in those republics, including the children of Chilian fathers, born in those countries of Bolivian and Peruvian mothers, in the barbarity with which that inhuman act was carried out, which caused the death of many unfortunate persons, and finally, in the confiscation of vast amounts of property in Bolivia, which was resorted to as a legitimate war measure.

The enemies of Chile, who take delight in giving currency to every kind of falsehood and absurd exaggeration to her detriment, never stop to think of what they have done themselves; and when their attention is called to those atrocities, particularly the confiscations, they have the hardihood to say that there have been other wars in which recourse has been had to such a measure. There have, indeed, doubtless been such wars in the centuries which preceded the eighteenth, but we deny that such a measure has been adopted since that time, for it is as barbarous as is torture and the severing of limbs from the human body.

Chile has not confiscated a single thing, however insignificant, belonging to her enemies, and, as regards precautionary measures, she has contented herself with ordering the names of Peruvian and Bolivian residents to be registered in a book, an inefficient measure, which has not even been enforced.

The enemies of Chile have been shrewd enough to circulate all the falsehoods that they saw fit, through the medium of the newspaper press of foreign countries, in order thus to arouse compassion in their behalf. To such an extent have they carried this policy, that they asserted that the Chilians had butchered eight hundred Italians in cold blood, after the battle of Miraflores. This extravagant statement was repeated by the newspapers of nearly the entire world, until the Italian Ministers at Lima and Santiago solemnly declared that not a single one of their countrymen had fought in the Peruvian ranks in that battle.

Equally shameless have been all the stories of atrocities said to have been committed by the Chilians.

The entrance of the Chilian army into Lima, after the battle of Miraflores, furnishes the brightest page that can be presented by the history of any nation, and was at the same time, the most humane act that could possibly be performed. The press of the entire world has applauded Chile for that act; but the Peruvians and Bolivians obstinately refrain from making any mention of that event, which was so glorious for a civilized nation, and persist in their malign task of characterizing the whole Chilian nation in a highly degrading manner.

CRUELTIES DURING THE OCCUPATION.

An effort has recently been made to obtain credence for the assertion that the Chilians have acted with cruelty during their occupation of the Peruvian coast. It appears that the charge is limited to the cities of Lima and Callao, because the occupation of the northern portion of the country is admitted by all to have been mild and humane.

Every man of ordinary common sense and of any experience knows that these charges are repeated in accordance with Voltaire's maxim " Lie, lie, something at least will be believed!" Chile has considered it as being beneath her dignity to circulate stories with regard to the blunders and crimes committed by her enemies, although she has been obliged to bear the slanders invented against her.

Nobody is ignorant of the mixture of races which exists in Peru and Bolivia, or of the ferocious character of some of those races. If nothing could be adduced in evidence of this save the murder of Presidents Balta and Morales, the horrible immolation of President Gutierrez and his brothers, that of ex-Presidents Pardo and Melgarejo, that of Colonels Gamio and Herencia Cevallos, etc., etc., ample proof would exist that no people can be found with more savage instincts in the entire Christian world. Their statements concerning what has been done by Chile are based upon false data, and are known to be destitute of truth by the many foreigners who have visited, or who reside in that country. Moreover, while statistics are accessible to everybody in Chile, revealing the miseries of human society, (as is the case in the United States,) it is impossible to look into any such mirrors in Peru or Bolivia.

In view of the national character of the Peruvians, and of the resistance which is naturally aroused by any foreign occupation, it is to be presumed that the acts of cruelty committed by the lower classes of that nation against the Chilian soldiers have been (as is the fact) numberless. And yet not more than three or four cases can be cited, even under military rule, in which criminals have been executed in a manner partaking in any way of atrocity, whereas any other army of occupation would have resorted a hundred times to that means of repression, which, under extraordinary circumstances, sometimes becomes necessary. Chilian soldiers have been sent to the gallows by the Chilian authorities, we do not remember whether once or twice, for offences which, in ordinary cases, would have sent their perpetrators to prison for ten years. This has been done in order to set the Peruvians an example of morality and justice.

All the complaints made by the Peruvians are, in a word, of such a nature as clearly to show that the Chilians, in order not to furnish ground for them, would have to be sisters of charity instead of enemies.

Those gentlemen, of course, pass over in silence and consign to utter oblivion the benefits, the benevolent acts, and the services rendered to public peace and tranquility for which they are indebted to the Chilian occupation. These *credits* are not entered in the account at all.

In the meanwhile, only those who have read nothing and heard nothing are ignorant of the fact that the Peruvians keep repeating, through all their public prints, that if the Chilians had evacuated Lima at any time during the occupation, Lima and Callao would have been sacked and burned by the guerrillas.

To invoke as credible testimony what is said in the newspapers by Peruvian correspondents, is a piece of folly of which no one, who is not either an enemy or an insane person, can possibly be guilty.

___

THAT CHILE HAS PROLONGED THE OPPRESSION AND RIGOROUS TREATMENT OF PERU.

One must be controlled by an excessive desire to misrepresent facts, in order to assert and repeat the above notorious falsehoods.

The most unequivocal proof that the charge is a malicious one, lies in the fact that the occupation of Lima and Callao has been considered by both natives and foreigners as the salvation of those cities.

It has been absolutely, physically and morally impossible, for Chile to treat with any even semi-legally constituted government. If she has treated with any of the guerrilla chiefs who claimed to exercise the supreme authority in Peru, the treaty would have been written in land or water. When Garcia Calderon acceptd the provisional presidency of Peru he knew perfectly well what were the requirements of the Chilians, and it is for that reason that his antagonists, Pierola and Montero, have declared him a hundred times to be a traitor to his country. He was lacking, however, in courage, in confidence in the destinies of his country, and in consistency in respect to the private promises which he had made, and preferred to encourage the groundless hope that some foreign power would espouse the cause of Peru. He then took the position that he would, under all circumstances, refuse to consent to any cession of territory, which position has been constantly declared by the government of the United States in its friendly policy towards the belligerents, to be adverse to the peace which is desired. That refusal is evident, not only from the letter authoritatively addressed by Mr. Hurlbut to Garcia y Garcia, Pierola's ministerial factotum, but atso from that addressed by Garcia Calderon himself to Lynch, when the latter prohibited him from performing jurisdictional act within the Chilian lines. That absolute refusal has fully justified the assertion which has been made by Chile in a contrary sense ever since the Arica conference.

The claim of the Peruvians and Bolivians that they must be the ones to settle the terms of peace, and that they have a right to fix the amount of the war indemnity, and the conditions on which it is to be paid, is something altogether devoid of common sense, and unworthy of any attention. Their claim that Chile's demands are exorbitant is the claim of an interested party, and cannot be seriously considered. If Chile had demanded the half of what she does demand, the same thing would have been said. We are not aware that the conditions announced by Chile to provisional ex-President Garcia Calderon have as yet been made public. All controversy in regard to this matter is, therefore, idle and useless.

Chile maintains, and advances incontestable reasons in support of her assertion, that she was provoked to take up arms. She also maintains that the acquisition of the territory which she claims is a necessary condition of security and defence, that it is something that is demanded by the peace of the continent, and that it will remove the causes which Peru and Bolivia had to injure her.

The refusal of the Peruvian leaders to treat on the basis proposed, has been, after a hundred vicissitudes, delays, embarrassments and disturbances, the secondary cause which has delayed the conclusion of peace.

The Peruvians and Bolivians, moreover, emphatically declare that the war is not yet at an end, although no more battles are fought, and they assert that Peru and Bolivia are now in a better condition for defense then ever, since they possess a more abundant supply of the sinews of war than they did before. What reason have they, then, for saying that Chile has unduly prolonged the occupation of the enemy's country, and what ground have they for appealing to the compassion of neutral nations?

The simplest understanding cannot fail to preceive the absurdity of the charge which we are now refuting. If the enemy is not conquered, and if he considers himself more powerful than he was before he lost his last battles, on what ground is the conqueror to be blamed or held responsible?

Chile thinks that she has triumphed, and that the time has come for her to treat with her antagonists as a conquerer with a vanquished foe. If her enemy does not think so too, he is wrong in considering himself beaten and prostrate, and still more so in begging neutral nations, who have no concern in a contest between two independent nations, to interfere in that contest.

If there is any doctrine that is universally condemned in the civilized world it is that of the old-fashioned interventious. To put that old political doctrine in practice again, after it has been everywhere rejected, would be to open up a vast field of battle in the world for all nations. If one Government should see fit to intervene for this or that reason, and in behalf of this or that interest, others would decide for different reasons to uphold this or that other interest, and mankind would thus become daily involved in universal war and wide-spread disaster.

The exploded doctrine of the balance of power is now discarded for ever; yet it is now claimed that intervention should be resorted to in the name of another doctrine which is quite as untenable as the former, and which is that of the theoretical interest of Democratic principles.

The independence and sovereignty of nations is the supreme reason that is opposed to the interference of neutral powers in wars with which they have no concern. If there ever could be a good reason for intervention, it would be in a case so exceptional, so extraordinary, so abnormal, arising from such historical causes and from so rigorous a community of collective interests that it would be extremely difficult to imagine one of such a character.

If the general welfare of humanity were to be considered, in the relatively unimportant question of the Pacific, the conclusion would be very easily reached that the nations of the world are interested in seeing Peru and Bolivia, which have ever been the theatre of the most shameful disturbances that results from anarchy and social corruption, pass under the control of a government which has set an example, in America, of order and stability in Republican institutions. Thus the New York Herald quite recently said that the true interest of this continent required the formation, in South America, of one great Republic, of Latin origin, just as there is one in the North of Anglo-Saxon origin.

This result would be promoted by the theory of universal interest, which Chile has no reason to take into the account. The only thing to which it is proper for her to call attention is the manifest fact that it is not for the Peruvians and Bolivians (whose disgraceful history they themselves have undertaken to write) to preach to neutrals about propriety and common interest in order to secure their aid. No foreigner can be interested in seeing his person and property brought under the dominion of confusion and anarchy, which have ever been the inheritance of those unfortunate countries.

RIGHT OF CONQUEST.

We have no acquaintance with anything, either in the present age or in the past, that is or has been called the right of conquest. Conquest has been a fact and nothing more than a fact imposed by force. Numberless wars have been waged, without any reasonable motive, for the purpose of conquering territory.

Those precedents, however, have no connection with the case now under consideration, in which there is no reason to mention the supposed right of conquest. The use of this empty word has no object but to interest frivolous or prejudiced minds.

Chile would never have made war against Bolivia and Peru, no matter what important considerations might have counseled her to remove the causes of disturbance existing in the North, if she had not been provoked. She bore, for a long time, all sorts of outrages and provocations, until at length her patience was exhausted.

When she had once conquered her enemies, she saw the legitimate result of her victory was the acquisition of what had been an apple of discord on the Pacific coast.

It is sought to give the name of conquest to that acquisition, which is, in strictness, but a partial indemnity. If, because the conquered party refuses to yield what is demanded of him, a territorial indemnity were to be considered as a conquest, it would only be necessary to persist, in all cases, in such a refusal, in order to cause every victorious nation to be regarded as seeking to exercise the right of conquest.

The Peruvians and Bolivians are not willing to consult the history of the United States in order to judge the cause of Chile, for it does not suit their purposes to do so. They seek subjects for their reflections in the Franco-Prussian war, and say that Prussia did not conquer Alsace and . Lorraine, because those provinces had belonged to Germany two hundred years before; yet in the very next breath they tell us that it is necessary for Germany to keep a standing army, and to deplete her treasury in order to keep the territories thus annexed under her control. The basis of their argument is therefore false, and the example to which some writers have pointed in order to justify the annexation to Chile, by way of partial indemnity, of the territory which she claims, is perfectly applicable to this case.

Among nations there are no tribunals to appeal to in order to enforce payment of what one owes to another. Nor are there any laws to fix the amount of an indemnity. That justice which is hypocritically invoked, is not absolute, nor can it be so, for that which is supremely just cannot be measured. Justice, whether enforced by courts or by nations among themselves, must be relative, since it is the application of human judgment to public or private affairs. Each one believes his cause to be just; and if, as in the case of the Peruvians and Bolivians, they are the ones who have placed themselves in a situation to be judged by their enemy, who, although humane and discreet, is still a conqueror, they have but to expiate their own errors. Chile will prove to the world that in the exercise of her right she has carried moderation even to excess.

Further on will be found a quotation from the writings of one of the four most eminent American publicists, which declares in favor of the right of appropriating territory by way of indemnity for losses suffered, when the conquered party is unwilling to come to terms. Twenty other authorities might be cited which uphold the same doctrine. We shall, however, for the present content ourselves with quoting the words of the eminent French writer, John Lemoine, in a recent article in the *Journal des Debats*, in reference to the course pursued by France in the North of Africa. Writing on the supposition that there is constant danger of hostility and attack from a neighboring enemy, he says : " Defense, in such a case, necessarily implies extension. It has not been through ambition of territorial aggrandizement or from love of conquest that the English have successively annexed the countries which now form their immense Indian Empire. They have been forced to do so by the law of self-preservation. . . . . It sometimes becomes necessary to annex, as the consequence of a war, even when no such design was entertained at the outset."

Payment in real property is not only a civil, but a natural right as well. Property is neither so sacred nor so inviolable but that it can be transferred to the creditor. The resistance of the debtor alone is utterly vain. The creditor has the right to sell the goods of the debtor, or to adjudicate them for himself. The debtor cannot resist the exercise of this right. And since among nations there is no supreme authority to regulate the order of procedure, it is clear that the creditor may demand payment either in money or in kind, as he may see fit.

These very elementary notions are not recognized by the enemies of Chile ; confounding honor and decorum with selfishness and caprice, they are willing to pay in money, which they do not possess, two or three times the amount which the ceded territory is worth to the State. Such an eccentricity cannot be agreeable to this nation, which is eminently one possessed of common sense.

This simple and daily-practiced right is the one which the Peruvians wish to condemn with the odious name of conquest. But since mankind are not so simple as to be deceived with jugglers' tricks, it is to be hoped that there is no American who, looking back on the history of his own country and on the acknowledged opinions of her statesmen, will allow himself to be deceived by the hypocritical pretences of Peruvians and Bolivians.

We have heard it said that the enemies of Chile claim that a large majority of the American public clamor for the intervention of this country in the conflict of the Pacific and we affirm that if the question were put to vote there would not be found one American in every hundred thousand who would care to entangle his country in foreign complications in order to defend the dulcineas of the Pacific, and that that one would be from an Eastern State, and would act in obedience to the promptings of personal interest. With regard to the press, it may be said that, excepting one or two uninfluential journals, all the New York dailies, as also those of Boston, Philadelphia and other large cities, have energetically condemned the intervention of the United States in South American affairs. All the larger dailies have fully recognized the following truths :

That the annexation of a more or less considerable portion of territory by the victor, as the result of a just war, and as a partial indemnity for losses suffered, is not a conquest, nor does it deserve the name in the sense in which this practice of the middle ages is condemned.

That the fanatical attachment to a piece of territory by those who never showed any love of country is something that cannot be seriously considered, but must be regarded as a farce for the entertainment of the spectators of both hemispheres.

That whenever they shall be left as the arbiters of their own destiny they will rend in pieces their country in fratricidal quarrels, as they have done almost continuously for the space of forty-five years.

That all modern wars, not alone that between France

and Prussia, have resulted in the occupation or acquisition of territory.

That Republican principles and institutions are not even remotely compromised by the war of the Pacific, which is relatively but a small incident in the great drama which is now being enacted by Republican institutions in America.

That the United States have no commercial or financial interest powerful enough to oblige them to set aside the noble trrditions of non-interference on which the power of this country is based, and that, on the contrary, the commercial and financial relations of the United States with Peru and Bolivia are so insignificant as not to be worth the paper that has been used in the consideration of the question.

That the independence and sovereignty of nations is too important an element to be subordinated to interests of small account, or to sentiments of sympathy and compassion.

That Peru and Bolivia have so poorly served Republican and Democratic institutions (which they have trampled upon and degraded), as to bar them from any claim to call to their aid the defenders of those grand principles.

That the Peruvians and Bolivians are seeking to create for their own benefit, a kind of universal socialism in imitation of the Quixotism of the Sixteenth Century, on account of which powerful nations should expiate the crimes of those Republics.

That all this far from being serious is comical in the extreme.

That the Monroe doctrine is being made a plaything for the amusement of triflers and fools.

That the tactics of the Peruvians and Bolivians in their attempts to interest the American public by arousing their greed, sordid ambition and all the lowest human passions, is in the highest degree offensive to the nation and should be spurned with contempt and disgust.

And the most unmistakable, conclusive and incontestable proof of the falsity and hypocrisy of the attachment which the Peruvians pretend to have for a particular section of country, is that all its ephemeral governments of recent date have been endeavoring to dispose of the Province of Tarapaca to foreign commercial companies rather than suffer it to be acquired by Chile, and that the Bolivians endeavor to excite the greed of adventurers by using their riches as an incentive to induce them to acquire the ownership of their territory. Additional evidence to the same effect is found in the fact that the Peruvians (we do not know whether the Bolivians have done the same), have offered to sacrifice their independence and annex themselves to the United States. What love, then, can they have for the soil of their country?

This feigned sentiment of patriotism is but a myth with which they would delude the too credulous or those possessed of too impressionable a nervous system.

The last proof of the Peruvians' love of country has been furnished by their offer to cede to the United States the port of Chimbote, to be used as a naval and coaling station, and to be thus converted into an American town. This offer the United States peremptorily refused. Had the Chilians asked for this port, which the Peruvians would so cheerfully give to the United States, there would have been heard a hue and cry about robbery, plunder, the infraction of the sacred rights of humanity, the trampling under foot of the rights of Republics, and the sovereignty of States.

RICHES OF BOLIVIA.

The Peruvians and Bolivians exaggerate the riches of their respective countries to a degree that is fabulous in the extreme.

But even if their representations were correct, they have nothing whatever to do with the question at issue. These riches are found either outside of the territory claimed by Chile, or are the property of private individuals or of joint stock companies. There is, therefore, no reason for bringing these riches into the account.

American interests in the saltpetre deposits are perfectly well guaranted by the Chilians, and it is not reasonable to suppose that it would even occur to any one to compare the Chilian guarantee with that of Peru or Bolivia. If the financial world is to judge of the merits of international guarantees, its decision has been given in favor of that nation whose credit is on a par with that of the most solvent European nation and against others which have no credit whatever.

The Bolivians assert that they have no European debts; but they forget the disaster brought upon them by the *Church Loan; and they forget also their debt to the Chilian Bank and to the Mejillones Railroad Company. The United States are well aware that they have been unable to obtain payment of the just debts which Bolivia has been owing them for many years.

The political *regime* of Peru and Bolivia bars the possibility of honest enterprise in those countries.

The dictatorships which continuously succeed one another in those countries, which may be said to be almost a normal part of their government, since, whenever a President is inaugurated as the constitutional ruler, he becomes a Dictator, constitute the most detestable and execrable

* A person of that name.

system known to the civilized world. The most odious tyranny and despotism are not to be compared with those dictatorships, which recognize neither God nor law. The Peruvians and Bolivians claim that murders are never committed on their highways, yet it is a fact that during the Chilian occupation no chilian soldier could leave his barracks without falling a victim to the cowardly hand of the Peruvian assassin.

Under these dictatorships and arbitrary governments there is no such thing as security of property. Congress is but the plaything of the despots. As proof of this we have only to read their own descriptions of themselves. They have upheld their own countries to universal abhorrence.

And are Americans now invited to carry their wealth and industry to such countries?

In order to give American citizens an idea of the security to business under the political administration of Bolivia, it is only necessary to refer them to some of their edifying transactions, and among others to those affecting the Antofogasta, Saltpetre and Railway Companies. But the narration would occupy time, and as judgment has already been passed upon the matter, there is no need of trying to convince those who are already convinced.

Nothing more need be said of a country which applauds and upholds the principle of confiscation in war as a highly enlightened one. Such a country should not be recognized in the community of Christian nations. Great Britain has, for many years, regarded Bolivia as being on a par with the tribes of the eastern coast of Africa.

FINANCIAL SCHEMES.

The enemies of Chile have opened a great market for financial schemes in this country in the hope of linking American interests with their own. They try to take advantage of the limited knowledge which prevails here with regard to South American affairs.

It will not be out of place here to remark that no speculative scheme of Chile has ever been brought forward in the financial or political market of the United States, and that there is no foundation whatever for the statement that the Chilians have attempted, or have even the remotest intention of proposing any transaction whatever in England, in connection with the saltpetre deposits, and this for the very simple reason that, according to the Chilian system, all the saltpetre deposits are property which is as sacred as are dwelling-houses, farms, mines, and other possessions which go to make up private property. Let this serve as a refutation of the malicious, or at least, inconsiderate assertion which we have frequently seen made by the press, to the effect that a Chilian guano and saltpetre scheme is being put upon the New York market. Those who credit such stories should understand that the Chilians relied entirely upon their own strength during the prosecution of the war, so they will rely upon their own strength for the promotion of their industrial and commercial enterprises.

The first scheme which suggests itself is the one which the Bolivian representative submitted to the State Department in the month of February last. The newspapers have frequently asked how the papers which furnished evidence for this scheme reached Chile, inasmuch as they had been sent by the Bolivian representative at Washington to his government. Americans and Chilians need not be asked how this came about, but the question should be asked of the Bolivians themselves. Three or four months after these documents had reached La Paz, a Bolivian sent them, as a present, to a Chilian residing at Valparaiso. This shows to what depth the honesty of Bolivian officials has sunk.

Be this as it may, what directly concerns us is that this scheme to which we refer and with which it was hoped to arouse the greed of the Americans, contains as many absurdities as it does words. It is to be doubted if even a lunatic could conceive a more preposterous scheme.

Peru and Bolivia have always tried to settle their difficulties by resorting to financial schemes, and these have plunged those countries, particularly the former, into poverty, discredit, corruption and anarchy. To be convinced of this fact we have but to read what they themselves have written and are writing in reference to the management of their public funds. A Peruvian in Arequipa recently wrote the history of the Meiggs' contracts, and it would be difficult to find a more disgraceful page in the history of any nation. The Peruvians would now have the United States use these very transactions as a pretext for interference when the interest which they have established can find no security and protection except under a respectable and honest government. It is not necessary to go into details in order to show the impracticability of the plan proposed by the representative to the business men of the United States. It will suffice to examine it in its principal bearings.

It is claimed in the first place that the saltpetre deposits of Bolivia and Peru belonged to the state. This claim is an absolute fiction, especially as regards those of Bolivia.

It is confidently asserted that the supply of saltpetre is inexhaustable, and that a profit of seven pounds ten shillings per ton may be realized upon it, which is simply absurd. It is necessary first to ascertain conclusively what is the amount of guano now remaining in Peru. What is its quality and its commercial value? All schemes not based upon such investigations are mere child's play and delusions.

Without entering into a detailed array of arguments and facts, which would not be within the scope of a paper like this, we may assert that all the guano worthy of consideration is to be found in the deposits known as Guanillos Pabellon de Pica, Bahia Independencia and Lobos Afuera. The quantity existing in these places is very much less than Dr. Cabrera supposes, and its quality is in general so poor that much of it cannot be exported.

So much with reference to the guano. As regards the saltpetre, it is an unpardonable error in persons in any way cognizant of the affairs of the Pacific coast to suppose that a monopoly could be formed from the deposits still said to belong to Bolivia and Peru. There exist, besides these, immense deposits at Taltal and Aguas Blancas, which have always belonged and still belong to Chile. The parties working these deposits have been able to compete (notwithstanding certain highly unfavorable conditions, among others the wretched condition of the roads,) with the producers of Antofogasta and Tarapaca. At present, however, they have railroad facilities, and are able to supply saltpetre at a lower rate than their competitors.

And in order to show the credit of Chile and the implicit confidence felt in it by foreign capitalists, it is only necessary to point to the fact that as soon as the construction of the road to Taltal was proposed in England the necessary capital was at one subscribed, and this, notwithstanding the fact that those who took the stock could not hope for a higher interest than $4\frac{1}{2}$ or 5 per cent. on their capital, as is the case in every legitimate investment.

It is to be expected that as soon as the companies which are now idle at Tarapaca shall resume work, competition will reduce the £5 14s. per ton, promised by Dr. Cabrera (which has never been the normal profit) to £1 and probably even less.

The plan proceeds to name the sum of thirty millions of dollars as the indemnity to be paid to Chile, whereas, the Peruvian Company fixes it at one million. Chile spoke of thirty millions at the Arica conference, which sum was to be payable to her in addition to the cession of territory which she demanded as far north as Camarones. But, as the world knows, matters have undergone a great change since then.

This plan, moreover, entirely ignores the immense sums due as interest at 8 per cent., payable in bills at 44 pence, which would be due on the saltpetre certificates almost from the date of their issue, for we have understood that interest was paid for but one-half year and that not upon all the certificates.

The general plan is based upon the supposition of a confederation between Peru and Bolivia, which is the greatest absurdity imaginable. No evil disposed spirit could contrive a more cruel kind of vengeance against those countries than to promote the formation of such a confederation, for from it would result a cat and dog quarrel, which would end in the ruin of both parties.

All who are acquainted with the history of those countries know that the hatred existing between the Peruvians and Bolivians is traditional, profound, and inextinguishable. More than a hundred documents published since the beginning of the war might be cited, which abound in recriminations, accusations, and mutual taunts. Any one that has conversed privately with Peruvians and Bolivians cannot have failed to be painfully impressed with the feeling of intense hatred manifested by them for each other, which feeling is the outgrowth of much bloodshed, of endless political intrigues and countless outrages. They accuse one another of treachery and cowardice, and thus it is that it has been impossible for the pretended Confederation to be cemented even by the alliance formed by the two countries against Chile.

Any American, English or French Company that should be deluded by a belief in this chimerical confederation, and induced to invest capital in those countries, would involve itself in such disasters as cannot be realized here, where no correct idea exists of the anarchy which prevails.

The other fundamental basis of the plan, which rests on the hypothesis that the saltpetre deposits are the property of the State, is absolutely false. The property of the Antofogasta Saltpetre and Railway Company is situated in Bolivia, as is also the Toco property, which belongs to the Chilian Government and to Mr. Charles Watson, of England. These are the two important deposits which owing to their situation, can be worked.

As to the saltpetre beds of Tarapaca, the matter is somewhat more complicated, but in reality, no less clear. It is true that President Pardo attempted to dispossess the owners of all the saltpetre deposits at Tarapaca of their property, compensating them for the same, and hence arose the debt which in the plan, is set down as amounting to twenty millions of dollars. President Pardo's idea was to dispossess whoever was unwilling to sell, and those who refused to do so were obliged to pay a heavy export duty. Four or five large establishments, with ample machinery, and from ten to fourteen offices, called *Paradas*, remained in the possession of their owners, and thus this measure of dispossession could never be fully arried out, and President Pardo was unable to realize in England the plans which he cherished with regard to the saltpetre of Tarapaca.

The management of the establishments thus appropriated was entrusted to a company under the control of the State. But the affair was so ill-conceived that, so far from being productive of any benefit, it entailed losses, and these, too, as a time when the Antofogasta Company was far from being as strong as it now is, when the deposits of Taltal and Aguas Blancas were just beginning to be worked.

A few days after the assassination of President Pardo, his own friends, who had blindly followed his lead in his plan of dispossessing the owners of the saltpetre deposits, presented to the Senate a bill for the abolition of that measure, which they stigmatized as wild, empirical, absurd and ruinous to the State. The scheme was at once abolished. President Pardo looked upon it as dead, and never again sought to resurrect it.

When Pierola succeeded to power he denounced all the acts of his enemy, Pardo, and, having had to occupy hsmself especially with matters connected with the purchase of saltpetre deposits, he issued a decree with regard to the Toco deposit, based on the ground that the State ought not to engage in industrial pursuits, that the measures adopted by Pardo had been highly detrimental to the nation, inasmuch as they had resulted in loss, and he consequently ordered the above mentioned deposit to be restored to Mr. Watson. We will not concern ourselves with the validity of this reversion. It is sufficient, for our own purposes, to state that thenceforth the scheme was regarded as null and void.

The various partial contracts, moreover, for the appropriation of saltpetre deposits by the State contained the express condition that they should become void if the parties failed to comply with their stipulations; and even if that condition had not been expressed, it was implied according to law. Peru failed to comply with any of the conditions which were principally that she should pay interest semi-annually, and the principal at the expiration of four years, in first-class bills of exchange, at the rate of forty-four pence to the pound. All the establishments were mortgaged to their former owners. The greater part of those establishments, certainly the most important ones, are to-day in the hands of their former owners, and the others soon will be.

An attempt to return to the system proposed by Mr. Pardo would give rise to a revolution which would involve most of the nations of the world.

The great importance of the United States is in a great measure due to their geographical isolation and to their policy of non-interference in foreign complications. This principle is recognized by the statesmen of the country and has lately been reasserted by that conscientious organ, the New York Times. And an effort is now being made to involve this Republic, by means of mercantile schemes and international guarantees, in complications fraught with endless mischief. And what shall we say of the bright suggestion Chile should take part in these wild schemes, and that the United States should furnish her their guarantees? This is left to the consideration of those who make a study of the hallucinations of the human mind.

What inducement, moreover, can there be for American capitalists to go to the ends of the world in the hope of such meagre gains as those held out by the plan now under consideration, even if such gains were possible? How and where would they reimburse themselves? It is hardly possible to imagine men foolish enough to risk a single dollar in so wild a scheme. Those who wish to invest in saltpetre enterprises may do so under the system of perfect liberty and absolute security offered by Chile.

The other scheme which was set on foot in opposition to that started in February, 1881, is that which is known as the Peruvian Company. This is *par excellence* a scheme of the lobby.

The plan proposed by this company is as absurd as the one already considered. It is difficult to know how to discuss it, because it is like an immense mountain of lard.

All the observations made in reference to the scheme of Doctor Cabrera are applicable to this, and even with greater force, inasmuch as the would-be monopoly includes only the Peruvian coast.

The " Peruvian Company " has published but a fourth part of the documents which would be necessary to enable us to pronounce judgment with regard to its imaginary claims.

No great knowledge of law is required in considering these same documents, and them only, to perceive, at a glance, where the weakness of the claim lies.

Setting aside the last executive act of Peru, which repudiated the claims of Landreau, (and, by implication, those of Cochet,) setting aside also what is understood by the Spanish laws as discovery—and leaving out of consideration the express provision that no appeal shall be had in these matters to diplomatic interference by any foreign nation, we observe that there is no formal instrument and written report showing that the pretended discoveries have placed previously unknown guano deposits in the possession of public officers. Everything has been left placed in lists prepared by the parties interested.

The fertilizing properties of guano were known to the ancient Peruvians, and it is ridiculous to claim that the utility of this fertilizer has been discovered since 1840.

The " Peruvian Company " does not present any matter of interest for a legislator, a statesman, or a merchant. It is best to leave it to make its own way against its rival, which was projected in February, 1881. Meanwhile, the world knows that Peru has not the means to pay what she owes to Chile. The hypotheses on which the possibility of such payment is based are quite as absurd as the two already examined, and it is now hoped that the United States will take a hand in schemes of patronage which could not be proposed to one of those monomaniacs, who, styling themselves the supreme regulators of human affairs, have caused the pages of the world's history to be written in blood.

Chile would not have made war against Peru and Bolivia on any consideration, and it is wholly unjust and illogical to suppose it credible that she contemplated conquest, because after she had become involved in a war into which she had been provoked by her enemies, she claims, according to universal custom, the just reward of her victories. What Chile now demands is that which belongs to her for many political, social, economical reasons, and which she is counseled to take by a due regard for her own safety, as well as for public order and the peace of the continent. These reasons will in time be made clear.

The considerations herein set forth are not to be taken as the defence of the cause of a nation, because nations are under no necessity to plead their cause before other nations which are their equals in respect to sovereignty and independence. Our object is simply to correct errors with regard to a matter which naturally cannot fail theoretically to interest friendly nations, and concerning which many thousand pages have been, and will hereafter be, written.

It may appear strange that money matters should be mingled with so serious a political question, but the wonder will cease when it is considered that the fact is beyond question that the attempt has been made to induce this government to lend its support to financial schemes to the end that they may furnish ground upon which to base the false and obsolete policy of intervention in South American affairs. It would not have been wise to have let these schemes run their course without a word of condemnation.

We will close with a word concerning the consignment of the guano found at Tarapaca to Messrs. Gibbs & Sons, and *concerning that guano only.* It is an error which must be in great part malicious, because it is a colossal one, to say that Chile has entered into a contract with Messrs. Gibbs & Sons, according to which they are to have the monopoly of the guano of Peru for a quarter of a century. This assertion is false, notoriously and wickedly false.

It is also to be observed that no one can assert that the guano of Peru will last twenty-five or ten, or even four years longer. As to that found at Tarapaca it is still more difficult to assert positively that it will continue to supply the markets of the world for the space of four or five years. All the world knows or may know, that the deposits of Bahia Independencia and of the Islands of Lobos Afuera are not comprised within the department of Tarapaca.

Having made these preliminary remarks let us explain what is meant by the consignment to Gibbs & Sons.

It is about two years since Mr. John Proctor came to Chile as the representative of a large syndicate of holders of Peruvian bonds, who thought that they had a direct claim to the guano at Tarapaca. After much exertion he obtained permission from the Chilian Government to take guano from those deposits on condition that a royalty of one pound ten shillings sterling, should be paid to the Chilian Government; that he should make the consignment to a first-class English house, and that this privilege should continue *only* as long as *the war lasted.*

After Mr. Proctor came Mr. Cave, the president of the committee, who secured the ratification of the previous permission, which was entirely spontaneous and optional on the part of Chile. As the syndicate was unable to get a first-class house to accept the consignment (since the mere mention that the affair was a Peruvian one, deterred everybody from engaging in it), the Chilian Government was obliged to lend the sanction of its respectability in order to obtain a consignee, and found one in the eminently respectable house of Gibbs & Sons.

There has been no contract for a monopoly or for a permanent consignment, nor has any arrangement been made for the disposal of any other guano than that of Tarapaca, and that only during the continuance of the war.

These facts are widely different from the statements to which the enemies of Chile are seeking to give currency, with a view to arraying the commercial interests of the United States against her.

The temporary cession made by the government of Chile to the holders of Peruvian bonds was the strongest proof that a nation could give of its generosity and high principle. Chile would willingly have made this concession to the United States if the creditors of Peru had been Americans. That measure has been severely criticised in Chile, on the ground that the government thereby consented to bolster up the Peruvian loan (which had fallen into such discredit), by thus sacrificing what would otherwise have been available as a war indemnity. Such, however, is Chile's course of proceeding.

In the meanwhile, from the islands of Lobos Afuera, a sale was made of 40,000 tons, which, according to the advices which we have received, will, if not entirely, at least for the most part, be sent to the United States.

Where, then, is the ground for just complaint or resentment against Chile ?

If any unpalatable truths are contained in the foregoing lines, this may be attributed to the fact that the Peruvians and Bolivians never speak of Chile without uncorking all the vials of their hatred and malignity against her.

Since writing the above, the despatches interchanged between the State Department and the United States Legation in Lima, with reference to the Peruvian Company, have been published.

These documents have left but a vague and undefinable impression. It is clearly seen that the matter has been treated too blindly ; that it has been sought to explore something in order to solve a gilded enigma, which has left everything in the same vagueness and obscurity as before, thus affording much for the impartial observer to think on.

The observations which at first sight, even without the need of careful examination are suggested by these documents, are the following :

That till now nobody knows how, when, or in what manner the so-called Peruvian Company has obtained possessions of the pretended claims of the Frenchmen, Cochet, and Landreau, and this is all the more important, inasmuch as it is necessary to establish the validity of those titles, since it is a matter of public note that Cochet and Landreau, or their heirs and successors, have disposed in Peru and France, at various times, portions of their pretended claims.

That the title on which the State Department finds valid or apparently acceptable reasons on which to base a claim is unknown. It is not known whether it is the discovery of a certain special method of treating the guano, or if it is the discovery of certain guano beds.

Those acquainted with the history and traditions of Peru are aware that even from the time of the Incas the children of the sun have used guano as a fertilizer, consequently it has not been necessary for any person, since the conquest, to teach its use. The exportation from Peru to Europe was begun without any intervention or participation, either on the part of Cochet or Landreau, by virtue of contracts made by the Peruvian Government with other persons. If Cochet or Landreau induced some friends, or those having any relations with them, to make any of these contracts, they can bring action against those persons whom they advised, but certainly not against Peru.

To lay claim as does the Peruvian Company to a right in the Chincha Islands, which were worked by the aborigines of Peru and then by the Spaniards from a remote antiquity is something which goes beyond the limits of credibility.

It is not known where the beds claimed to have been discovered by Landreau are situated. There never has been an act drawn up of these discoveries, nor is it known whether the supposed discoverer ever laid claim to it, or if even a single ton was ever shipped from these imaginary beds.

All the suppositions that are formed in regard to the matter are baseless.

Whenever a person makes any scientific or industrial discovery, he will acquire a patent or such conventional premium in coin, as the party profiting by such a discovery, or to whom the revelation of the idea is made, may think fit to give; but never can he aspire to a right over material objects which are not his own.

There is on the other hand no antecedent which can lead us to suppose that Cochet or Landreau ever made scientific or industrial discoveries with reference to Peruvian guano or saltpetre.

If the discovery of material objects is involved, it is necessary to hand them over in an inventoried form or in such a way as will afford a guarantee or which may possess judicial value.

There exist in Tarapaca the deposits of Guanillos and Pabellon de Pica, neither of which are included in the list of the pretended discoveries of Cochet and Landreau, but on the contrary they are excluded, the one implicity and the other impliedly in the prospectus of the Peruvian Company, which has been given by its agent to the Secretary of State and to the United States Minister at Lima.

But above this consideration, there is one of right, which consists in fixing the sense, the extent and true meaning which is attached by the Spanish laws to the expression, " discovery of hidden and unknown things," (" *descubrimientos de cosa oculta y desconocida.*") Has an investigation been made by the State Department with reference to this matter before putting forth opinions with regard to the admissibility of such a claim?

The Peruvian Company has selected among thousands those documents which have been most advantageous to itself, and laid them before the public. They will suffice for the condemnation of its pretensions against Peru.

Since diplomatic action in this matter is condemned, and since it is an elementary principle of law that any one may renounce any right which benefits him, even when statutes, with regard to public order are concerned, whoever makes a disinterested and critical study of the matter in question must attach decisive importance to it, and consider the acts of the Peruvian Government as putting an end to the claims of Landreau.

We do not believe that an instance can be cited in the history of diplomacy of an official demand being made when such a demand was precluded by the terms of the contract. England has gone further, because it has declared at various times that, since its citizens are free to seek their residence where they may, and under such laws as they may choose, they have no reason to call on their government for diplomatic aid whenever they may suffer or think they suffer harm in the country where they reside.

But the most singular part of the affair is that setting aside the Cochet claim, which seems to be condemned as absurd, it is not known what is claimed for Landreau, nor what is the interest of Landreau's brother, who became an American citizen, in the Peruvian concerns of his French brother. Yet the whole affair is considered as if all the claim belonged to the naturalized citizen of America.

The State Department admits the principle that whenever an American acquires the property or rights of a foreigner he also acquires the advantages and disadvantages which belonged to the grantor. Consequently, since it has never been claimed that the Americanized Landreau ever discovered any saltpetre deposits in Peru, the following maxim is applicable to his case, that, "If American citizens purchased an interest in such claim, they purchased nothing more than the original claimant possessed. They did not purchase the good offices of this government ―― " ― This maxim applies to the claim of Cochet as well.

Whatever may be the question in reference to Peru, it does not concern Chile in any way. The one is a matter entirely independent of the other, and since no one can claim rights *in re* in any part of territory or its accessories in Peru, there is no reason whatever, for entangling Chile in matters or claims, personal or *ad rem*, of foreigners against Peru. There is between Chile and these foreigners not even the slightest relation of mutual rights.

We can assert, likewise, that we have no knowledge that any citizens of France, England or any other country, would in any way interfere under the pretext of having any of their personal claims considered in the stipulations of the treaty which will be arranged between Chile and Peru.

The Peruvian Company resembles one of the many fabulous quarrels about ancient inheritances, which occur every now and then, over runningthe bureaux of lawyers, and are looked upon everywhere as mere schemes. Even now there is an illustration of this in the fuss that is being made of some hidden millions of Confederate funds, which, to our knowledge, has not interested any person of sense.

The claim in question tends to convert Peru into a colony or American factory, because its colossal importance absorbs, as the Peruvian Company itself claims, with Christian modesty, all the natural riches of the country.

In closing, we would call the attention of the public to the last hypothesis, that has been published which is, that in the treaty of peace that shall be concluded between Chile and Peru, the Laudreau claim ought to be considered according to the judgment which the Peruvian tribunals may pass without any reference to the judicial authority of Chile.

In order to have it condemned in every particular it is only necessary to state that this hypothesis is based on the supposed existence of a right in favor of Landreau.

MANIFEST

Ministry of Foreign Affairs,
Santiago, April **12, 1879.**

Mr. Minister.—Annexed to the present note you will find a copy of the official gazette of Chile, from which you will learn the authorization conferred on my government by the high authorities of the State, to declare war against Peru, and conduct it to an end by all the means recognized by the rights of nations, and with all the resources at the disposal of the country.

By order of H. E., the President of the Republic, I inform you of the grave causes that have led to this unavoidable, though lamentable, resolution, which breaks old ties that Chile has always endeavored to strengthen.

The government, in whose name I have the honor of speaking, flatters itself with the hope that the calm judgment of that represented by Y. E., will duly appreciate the conduct that Chile has observed in this emergency—as foreign to her character and tradition, as contrary to her dearest interests.

The special characteristic of this country, the constant tendency of its foreign policy, and even its social and economic necessities, have withdrawn it from all spirit of adventure, and have stimulated it to maintain the most friendly relations with all nations. Chile lives by peace and industry; requires as a prime element of its prosperity, foreign immigration; and possessing a vast territory, only partially fertilized by the rude labor of its sons, requires more that any nation, foreign and internal tranquility.

The latter has been obtained, thanks to the frank adoption of a system by which all the public powers emanate from the national vote; and clearly is it proved, by the history of many years, that it has always endeavored to avoid conflict with foreign nations. The republic can show with legitimate pride that it has never been sparing of its blood or resources whenever it has been embarked in a noble cause, and much less when to it has been united the interests of this continent; but it can also declare with no less satisfaction that, though always ready to defend outraged rights, it has systematically avoided all provocation, even under circumstances that would have authorized it. Only a few months ago it gave a new proof of the traditional character of its policy, by submitting to the honorable solution of arbitration, an old and vexed question, which it sustained against a neighboring power, although it had to yield to the uncertainty of a sentence, rights to which the national sentiment attached great importance. From this it will be easy for Y. E., to deduce that Chile, in forgetting its historic conduct and the necessities of its situation, has done so only by the irresistible force of evident justice and in obedience to the clearest demands on its dignity.

My government very recently complied with its duty in manifesting to those with whom it has the pleasure of maintaining cordial relations, the circumstances which obliged it to declare at an end the treaty existing with Bolivia, and to occupy the territory lying between parallels 23 and 24 S. lat.

Subsequently, and without previous declaration of war, the President of Bolivia issued a decree emanating from his single will, by which he expelled Chilian citizens from that state, confiscated their property, and sequestrated the products of the industry and capital of this country.

It is unnecessary to recapitulate the bonds uniting the two nations, confirmed by solemn treaties, never respected by our neighbors; unnecessary to repeat that since 1866 till the occupation of Antofogasta on February 14, of this year, my government, by a series of concessions, more or less valuable, had arrived at the last sacrifice in order to maintain peace.

If Chile has been forced into war, it is not through its own act, but is the unavoidable consequence of the extraordinary conduct observed by the Government of La Paz. This, on one hand, declined to fulfil the treaty of 1874, in virtue of which, and by whose sole title it occupied conditionally the territory whose possession was transferred by the treaty mentioned. On the other hand it refused the honorable resource of arbitration, pretending to constitute itself absolute judge of the interpretation and practical application of the rights and duties established by the mutual sanction of both nations.

From whatever point of view the severest impartiality may consider the irregular proceedings of the Bolivian authorities, we feel convinced that the friendly powers whose opinion we so much esteem will recognize, in homage to the strictest justice, that the situation imposed on Chile by a will not its own, indicated one sole course as possible in the protection of its dignity.

My government, nevertheless, in spite of antecedents that perhaps should have indicated a different course, wished to limit itself to pointing out the natural consequences of the rupture of the treaty of 1874. If it be undeniable that before the treaty of 1866, the territory comprised between parallels 23 and 24, belonged to Chile by right and by the constant exercise of veritable possession ; if it be true that it was ceded to Bolivia by the treaty of 1874 on the emphatic condition that no new taxes should be levied on Chilian industry and capital, and if in indeed it is the melancholy truth proved by public documents of the Bolivian Government, that turning a deaf ear to all remonstrances, it ceased in truth to impose taxation, but rendered illusory the right of property recognized by its own laws, it was necessary on the part of Chile to replace things in the state in which they stood before the extraordinary violation of the treaty mentioned.

This violent act of Bolivia was necessarily followed by the occupation of the consideration ceded on the ground of non-fulfilment of the conditions. This sufficiently explains the landing of our troops at Antofogasta, so that in attributing to this the character of a belligerent act, the antecedents of the conflict are deliberately disregarded. In order to avoid the occupation Bolivia possessed the means open to the commonest honesty—namely, promising to respect the treaty of 1874. This would have been the course of a civilized nation, for no reasoning, no protest, can defend the unjust sentence Bolivia claimed to give in the question ; to retain the territory it owed to the liberality of Chile, and at the same time to break the fundamental condition of the concession.

It is painful, but at the same time indispensable, to bring to the memory of friendly powers another evident reason that my government could have wished not to reveal, out of respect to a State of the same origin. Official documents, and still more, the private history of Chilian industry on the coast between 23° and 24° S. lat., are witnesses that cannot be refuted, to the fact that since 1866 to the date of the occupation of Antofogasta, the Bolivian Government appears to have conceived, organized, and put in practice an inflexible system of persecution against the development of Chilian enterprises, which have been the only origin and the principal element of the wealth of that locality, never suspected and never stimulated by the private industry or national protection of Bolivia.

The capital of this republic, and that developed under the protection of our laws without distinction of nationality, being embarked in costly speculations, my government could not view with indifference the adoption by Bolivia of special measures tending to place Chilians in an exceptional situation. Soon after the treaty of 1866, and then after that of 1874, the painful certainty was realized that in Bolivia no idea existed of individual guarantees. Taxes were imposed under the pretext of municipal rates ; disgraceful punishments were inflicted by the authorities on citizens of this republic, and finally, a Chilian enterprise for the working of nitrate beds, authorized by the Bolivian Government, afforded a pretext for a law irreconcilable with the most essential stipulation of the treaty of 1874.

My government could not abandon its citizens to Bolivian caprice, and less to the discretion of its subalterns; and the official documents inserted in the reports of the Ministry of Foreign Affairs since 1866 render unnecessary any additional proof, that since then till now it has been impossible to retain the action of the Bolivian authorities.

These precedents showed sufficiently that the occupation of Antofogasta was urgently required, through the violation of the treaty; and my government found itself under the necessity of ordering it for the protection of interests and persons threatened by measures which respected no rights whatever.   •

The occupation effected on February 14 could not be considered as a declaration of war, and still less as a threat on the part of my government against the sovereignty of Bolivia. Nor was it reasonable to suppose that the Cabinet of Santiago intended to modify the geographical limits of the neighboring nations. In this conflict, which never would have arisen if even a show of respect had been evinced for the spirit and letter of treaties, what this republic has aimed at from the beginning, with the greatest frankness, was to defend its national rights and protect private property. Before 1866 we possessed effectively up to parallel 23. By the treaty of that year we accepted the exportation in common up to parallel 25, and subsequently we fixed the limits of Chile at 24°, on condition that the neighboring republic should exempt our industry from any new exaction.

The situation of the two republics seemed to be clear enough. Chile renounced its effective possession up to lat. 23° S.; Bolivia ceded its fantastic pretentions up to lat. 24° and both countries, respecting the fact that Antofogasta, Mejillones, Caracoles, and Salinas were of Chilian creation, agreed to guarantee the freedom of the industries established in those regions. This undoubtedly was an immense sacrifice to Chile, considering that she not only ceded to Bolivia, a territory in dispute, but also a large area over which her title could not have been questioned for a moment.

The antecedents of the treaty of 1866 and the negotiations which resulted in that of 1874, are the most evident proofs that Chile, far from desiring the extension of its limits recognized under the colonial *regime*, only sought an arrangement that permitted the untrammelled exercise of Chilian industry: notwithstanding the appropriation by Bolivia of the territory that we possessed.

It is unnecessary to dwell upon the right of a sovereign state to claim from another with which it contracted the fulfillment of its stipulations, and the no less indisputable right to employ the means of enforcement which the law of nations has adopted. Although the proceeding of my government was open to no objection, considering that the conflict with Bolivia in no way affected Peru, we wished to give the latter a proof of our friendship by informing it fully of whatever transpired, previously calling its attention to the necessary results of a groundless complication.

The Lima Cabinet knew, therefore, everything concerning the negotiations at La Paz; it could appreciate the tenacious resistance opposed to the conciliatory proposals of our chancery; and it also knew that such proposals were replied to by unheard-of acts of violent spoliation. In spite of this, that Cabinet, so zealous for the peace of America, which has assumed at the eleventh hour the charge of Bolivia, could find then—when an opportunity offered for it to fulfil its duty—not a single word nor course whatever to avert a conflict in which it may now be said Peru represented a secret *role* by no means in conformity with its much talked-of highmindedness.

It was our duty then to confide in the loyalty of Peru; still more, we had the right to demand it, either on the ground of a sincere friendship, or as a slight return for the blood of our citizens and our treasure spent in giving that country a nationality, and defending it at the price of our own ruin.

It was natural for us to give faith to the professions of neutrality which the Peruvian Government transmitted to us through our plenipotentiary; and to consider as friendly the intimation given us by that Cabinet, that until war was declared it must permit the passage of Bolivian troops through its territory, in virtue of a previous treaty.

There were, however, various antecedents which contradicted in a great measure the declarations that with full knowledge of circumstances we now may stigmatize as insidious. The President of Peru did not hesitate to express his fears for the pressure that might be brought to bear in an opposite sense by a reckless popular opinion. ' He hinted at the not improbable event of the action of the authorities being interfered with, and recognized the influence of certain circles whose disaffection to Chile is only founded on the childish jealousy with which our prosperity is regarded.

This caused my government to observe an attitude of vigilant expectation. According to the rules regulating the relations of friendly powers, it would have been rash to provoke a definitive situation; but according to the claims of our own responsibility, we were bound to prepare for any emergency.

This explains the reception accorded to the extraordinary legation from Peru which arrived at Santiago at the beginning of March, with words of peace and conciliation.

The nature of the complication with Bolivia did not exclude the possibility of some arrangement, as it was not our desire to make war unnecessarily. My government, however, believed that all mediation under the existing circumstances was inopportune; that it had even been so when on a previous occasion it had been offered by the *charge d' affaires* of Peru; and that the Cabinet of Lima had lost the occasion of interposing its friendly offices, even if it had at any time professed them.

When the government of La Paz showed itself deaf to all remonstrance ; when its only argument was decrees violatory of the treaty of 1874; when it replied to pacific indications by the enforcement of the law of 1878 which implicitly abrogated its recent pledges to Chile ;—then indeed mediation would have been practicable, supposing that Peru had possessed the real character of an honorable mutual friend.

Believing firmly that mediation for the moment was groundless, my government yet considered that such belief was not incompatible with hearing the ideas of the Peruvian Government transmitted by its representative, Don Jose Antonio de Lavalle. At the preliminary conference held by the undersigned with Senor Lavalle, it appeared that the object of the mission was to exchange ideas and make general observations on the Chileno-Bolivian question. As then the belief became more pronounced in the existence of a secret treaty of alliance, concluded in the year 1873 between Peru and Bolivia, it seemed advisable to interrogate Senor Lavalle concerning an event of such importance; and as at the same time an unusual activity was observable in the army and navy of Peru, explanations were demanded as to the significance and object of such preparations.

Senor Lavalle gave the following reply :

" That he had no knowledge of the treaty alluded to; that he believed it had no existence; that it could not have been approved by the Congress of 1873, because the legislature being biennial till the constitutional reform of 1878, that assembly did not meet in that year ; and that he was sure it was not approved on the following years, during which he had the honor of presiding over the diplomatic committee of Congress, at which such negotiation would necessarily have had to be discussed. But nevertheless, as since his arrival in Chile, he had heard the existence of this treaty spoken of, he had asked instructions from his government, which he would communicate as soon as they were received."

Respecting the belligerent attitude which Peru commenced to assume, its representative attributed it to the special condition of its territory, and to the necessity of preventing its violation by the operations of the belligerents, which it was reasonable to anticipate, as the Bolivians had invaded it even in cases of internal commotion.

These explanations were not tranquilizing, because they were not conclusive, and confirmed my government in the conviction that it would be necessary to solve so equivocal a situation before the Cabinet of Lima itself, and even without knowing its antecedents, instructions were immediately sent to our minister at that capital, to ask for a prompt declaration of neutrality.

The Cabinet of Lima, as I have already had the honor of stating to Y. E., declared to our representative, verbally, that it would be neutral in the conflict with Bolivia, and that such resolution would remain in suspense until the declaration of war was officially announced.

On March 14, our minister in Lima informed my government that the Charge d'affaires of Bolivia had made known to the diplomatic corps there resident that his country was at war with Chile. and on the same day orders were sent Senor Godoy to demand the declaration of neutrality. It was asked for, in moderate terms, on the 17th of the same month, and the Peruvian chancery, replying on the 21st, referred to instructions that would be transmitted to its Envoy Extraordinary in Chile, without explaining the reasons which induced it to delay the solution of a legitimate right which gave no margin for further explanations. The disloyal evasion of Peru was unacceptable even to the least suspicious judgment, and for this reason my government informed Senor Godoy on the same day that it did not admit of such a tardy course being adopted; that it insisted on claiming its right in Lima itself; and that it now not only asked Peru to define its attitude, but demanded a frank explanation as to the object of its armament, and substantial guarantees for the future, in the event of any probable contingency.

Such a demand was fully justified. The extraordinary mission of Senor Lavalle, at such a critical moment, only served to satisfy us as to his ignorance of subjects of immense importance ; and at the same time the government of Lima had to be reminded that it had confessed itself impotent to fulfil its duty, and that an explosion of hate as profound as unreasonable against this republic, had burst forth among the people of the pretended mediator.

The moment had therefore arrived to dissipate all doubt. My government, sensible of the responsibility weighing upon it, and being aware of the extent of the right of self-defence before an ill-defined neutrality that was arming in every haste, did not hesitate to give its demands the pressing nature that the gravity of the situation demanded.

On the said 21st of March, Senor Godoy communicated to my government the result of that step, but the defective telegraphic transmission necessitated the rectification of the dispatch, which from various causes could not be effected before the night of the 24th. His note had not been replied to in writing, but in verbal conference he was given clearly to understand by the government of Peru that it was impossible for it to assume a neutral attitude, owing to the existence of a treaty of alliance with Bolivia. In spite of the importance of this declaration, that government insisted on Chile abiding by the explanations of the l'eruvian envoy; and exhibited, with an impassiveness at variance with the simplest demands of honor, the desire of postponing the solution of the problem.

Nevertheless, my government, obedient to the respect which it has always professed towards the opinions of other nations, and desirous of avoiding the reproach of hastiness, by the omission of any essential requisite to establish clearly the situation of Peru, endeavored to obtain explicit and exact explanations.

On the said 24th of March peremptory instructions were sent to our minister at Lima. According to them he was to insist that the question of neutrality should not be discussed in Chile; that we demanded the immediate and guaranteed suspension of the armament, and the production of the secret treaty, inquiring if it was approved in due form, and if Peru was disposed to abrogate it immediately and give us the requisite explanations for having negotiated in secret, while on terms of friendship with us, a treaty showing want of confidence in and even of hostility towards Chile.

Such were our last demands and their just foundations. Our representative in Lima, putting them into prompt execution, conferred verbally with the head of the Peruvian Government and the members of his Cabinet.

The result of these conferences was the following declarations, which suffice without any comment to show the international policy of a government allied till then with us by a treaty of friendship offered by Chile when the ancient masters of Peru imposed on it a humiliating vassalage.

The Cabinet of Lima, without a tinge of shame, undeterred by recent events, without even the frankness which occasionally excuses great faults, tranquilly answered our minister:

1. That it would not declare nor assume an attitude of neutrality, though with an incomprehensible logic it offered, nevertheless, on its already violated word, to suspend its warlike preparations.

2. That the secret treaty with Bolivia—a shameful net spread for our friendship—was duly completed for a long time past.

3. That that treaty, whose hidden existence was the best proof of its bastard nature, had to be kept secret in accordance with one of its articles, calculated cunningly against the friend of many years, the ally in trouble, the saviour in the two great crises of the nation that with such a monument testified its gratitude; and

4. That a copy of this singular treaty had been remitted to Senor Lavalle; but on the understanding that it should only be read to us, doubtless to satisfy our curiosity to know a negotiation whose like can scarcely be found in the darkest records of diplomacy.

It is not surprising that the Cabinet of Lima had the assurance to insist, with all the appearance of seriousness, on the possibility of the continuance of the pending negotiations?

If all this was not war, such as is understood by civilized nations, it signified the same thing, under the transparent disguise of the mediator, who assumed the double part of a friend when he was an interested belligerent.

The secret treaty of February 6, 1873, needs no lengthy examination to ascertain its object; and the reserve in which it has been maintained confirms, in the least suspicious mind, the conviction that it was entered into solely as a means of security for the fiscal egotism of Peru in its pecuniary troubles, and to aid the schemes of the government of Bolivia, a perpetual conspirator against the treaty of 1866. In 1873 neither Peru nor Bolivia was threatened by the remotest danger of territorial dismemberment; and much less could it be foreseen that Chile cherished such idea, seeing that it had granted to Bolivia whatever that republic demanded in the convention of 1866—applauded by the Bolivian people as a splended manifestation of Chilian generosity.

The treaty of 1873 owed its origin—hidden as a shameful act—to the measures adopted by Peru at that epoch, to justify one of the most audacious and cruel spoliations witnessed by countries submitted to a *regime* of common respect towards the industry of all nations.

Peru desired to monopolize and appropriate the nitrate works; and in order to sustain its daily diminishing credit, adopted the supreme measure of ruining an industry to satisfy a fiscal voracity that could not satisfy itself with the' ordinary resources of a country that has lived, thanks to its territorial wealth, in complete obliviousness of economy and labor.

Y. E. cannot be ignorant of the situation of these three republics in February, 1873; and, in fact, only by the reason I have just indicated can be explained the existence of the treaty of that year, entered into in provision of acts that nobody threatened to realize—that could not be realized while the treaty of 1866 existed; and when in no case was it possible to anticipate that Chile or any other nation would threaten the integrity of Bolivian territory, or the never-disputed sovereignty of Peru within its recognized limits.

It is evident that Peru sought in the treaty of 1873 to protect the financial measures it meditated against an industry that in any commonly scrupulous country would have had the right to develope itself freely. What it desired was to strengthen the nitrate monopoly, without considering the sum invested in that industry; for in vain are antecedents of any kind scraped up to justify the belief

—not probable, but even possible—of any aggression against the independence or dominion of the contracting powers.

Knowing the respective situation of these countries, the secret treaty of which I have spoken was either wholly useless, or it possessed an ulterior design that events have shown to be the real one. Neither Bolivia nor Peru could fear the perturbation of their sovereignty by any of the surrounding nations; so that the alliance is explainable by much less elevated motives, and which were purposely intended to embarrass the action of my government in exacting the fulfilment of the treaty we had celebrated with Bolivia, and to provide against the consequences of the indignant clamor of Chilian citizens, despoiled by the despotic hand of the monopoly established in Tarapaca.

As a last analysis, the Peru-Bolivian convention was for Peru the cold calculation of a trader; and for Bolivia a vote of indemnity which covered the previous violations and future infractions of the agreement of 1866. The monopolizing interest of the former republic and the international ill-faith of the second, found their faithful expression in that document, whose celebrity will be as lasting as the condemnation which the honest conscience of every civilized people will attach to it.

And this, Y. E. will observe as an original lesson of diplomatic loyalty, was on the eve of adjusting the treaty of 1874; when Chile, without necessity, and only in homage to peace, being able to exact the fulfilment of the treaty of 1866, agreed to renounce its recognized right to the territory between 24° and 23°.

There is even yet something more worthy of observation. Article 3 of the secret convention reserves to each party the qualification of the *casus fœderis*. The 8th establishes as a solemn pledge, to avert war as far as possible, employing conciliatory means to avoid a rupture, and among them arbitration.

Peru therefore possessed the fullest liberty of action for deciding if the time for an alliance had arrived. It could and ought to have considered the object and character of the operations undertaken by my government; and more than one opportunity presented itself for offering its mediation, when it assisted as a mute witness to the negotiations whose logical results it could not otherwise than foresee. It is not therefore unwarrantable to impute to the Cabinet of Lima, the deliberate intention formed long before of assuming the character of a belligerent. For this reason it manifested a decided inclination for neutrality even whilst it armed with unusual rapidity; for this it sent us a legation which claimed to be without instructions on the cardinal points of its mission; for this, whilst it delayed the replies asked by our representative, it sent urgent orders to Europe for new war material.

All this would merit, on the part of any power disinterested in the conflict, qualifications too severe for my government to repeat here, out of respect for that of Y. E. The nations whose worthy representatives, I have the honor to address, will observe by the accompanying documents, that even accepting as obligatory the secret treaty of 1873, the Peruvian Government was free from any pledge. That of Bolivia refused the arbitration referred to in article 8 of the secret treaty, as it did in the treaties celebrated with Chile; and the *casus fœderis* had not occurred, inasmuch as Chile stated, and repeated frequently, that it did not intend to conquer a hair's breadth of Bolivian territory. Peru not only could, but should have observed the strictest neutrality, even without violating the secret stipulations entered into with Bolivia; because these are founded on the existence of a threat against territorial integrity, which was never thought of on our part; and because they also fix as an indispensable precedent to the *casus fœderis* the previous recourse to arbitration.

The explanations given by Senor Lavalle, far from attenuating, strengthened more clearly, if that be possible, the terminant spirit of the treaty of 1873. How accept the trifling excuse that it contained a generic stipulation, not directed at Chile, whilst it is carefully hidden from her knowledge? If the treaty meant a general guarantee against any advance of a foreign power, why was the co-operation of Chile not sought, which has given more than one example of being the first to contribute, with its men and its wealth, towards the maintenance of the sovereignty of nations of a common origin?

It was still more inconceiveable that Peru should inform us by its envoy that the reserve of the treaty arose from one of its conditions, fearing our susceptibilities might be wounded if it proceeded to act as mediator while informing us of its relations with one of the belligerents.

To discuss such allegations would be merely to tire your patience, and is doubly unnecessary, inasmuch as Peru, from the beginning of the conflict has done everything in its power to elude any explanation relating to the secret treaty.

My government needed no extraordinary effort to ascertain, from the acts and declarations related, what was the position that Peru preferred to assume, what were the rights, and more than all, what were the duties that were consequently imposed.

. The mediator offered himself, backed by an army whose rapid assembly testified to the prevision of proximate conflicts; manned his navy, and whilst uncertainly stammering words of impartiality, allowed to transpire the engagement of a belligerent duly sealed.

It was Peru, which, if it did not declare war first, with the frankness of a noble resolution, commenced it first—and what is worse, a war hidden and sheltered under false protestations of friendship.

Chile has never forgotten the course marked out by the patriotism of its sons, the energy strengthened by the conviction of violated justice and its historic name among civilized nations. It is Peru that has plotted and desired war, let Peru therefore be charged with the responsibility, whilst Chile delivers its future to the protection of God, to the stout hearts of its citizens and to the just opinion of enlightened nations—I have, etc.

ALEJANDRO FIERRO.

MEMORANDUM

DELIVERED BY THE MINISTER OF CHILE TO THE SECRETARY OF
STATE, STATING THE ACTUAL CONDITION OF AFFAIRS
ON THE PACIFIC COAST.

I take the liberty to address to your Excellency, Mr.
Secretary of State, the present informal memorandum with
regard to affairs on the Pacific coast, for the purpose of
explaining to you the present state of the question, and of
showing how it is that, in the published reports which are
readily credited by some persons, there are glaring contra-
dictions, egregious errors, a total want of knowledge of
the fact, and no little evil intent.

In verbal conferences, important points are apt to escape
unnoticed, and it is not always possible to maintain unity of
reasoning in the development of an extensive and complex
matter.

My government is most deeply interested in having that
of the United States correctly informed as to affairs on the
Pacific coast, that it may be enabled duly to appreciate the
upright and prudent policy of Chile, and thoroughly to
understand those events which are yet to come.

CHILE AND PERU.

You are better aware, Mr. Secretary, than any other
person, of the immense difference which exists between the
antecedents and, social, political and material life of these two
countries. There is no need of stopping to express opinions
with regard to these matters.

Nor is there any need of consuming time in relating the
history of the origin of the war. The only thing that it is
proper to mention in this connection is that, in the senti-
mental crusade which is now being carried on in behalf of

Peru, it is attempted to present that country in the light of
an innocent victim to its attachment to Bolivia. The truth
is that Bolivia would never have dared to throw down the
glove to Chile had it not been for the stimulus and encour-
agement afforded by Peru. The policy of the latter country
has been traditionally hostile to us, especially since 1838,
when Chile went to aid in freeing that nation from the yoke
of the Bolivian despot, Santa Cruz. Of late years Peru's
cherished plan has been to monopolize the trade in saltpetre,
not considering that that substance exists in immense quan-
tities on the coast of Chile, the possession of which has never
been disputed, and having that plan in view, it effected
seizures of property at Tarapaca, which caused the ruin of
many Chilian citizens, and deprived Valparaiso of its proud
position as the emporium of the saltpetre trade, and which
was on the point of plunging Chile into financial ruin.. Saltpetre, that is to say the undivided control of the production
of that article, has been the direct source of all the machina-
tions of Peru against Chile. As the same article existed
likewise in Bolivia, the rulers of Peru obtained, by indirect
and underhanded means, control of an extensive district
known by the name of Toco; and as the immense deposit
owned by the Chilian Company called the "Antofogasta
Saltpetre and Railway Company," still remained there,
Peru suggested to Bolivia to endeavor to ruin that powerful
corporation. It was thought that Chile, which had manifested no hostile disposition for more than thirty years,
which had meekly borne all the insults that had been put
upon her, which was entirely unarmed, and which, moreover, was involved in a critical complication with the Argentine Republic, would patiently allow herself to be insulted
and imposed upon. From that cabal arose the disingenuous
acts of Bolivia, which were the immediate causes of the
war. Peru induced Bolivia to conclude with her the treaty
of alliance of 1873 against Chile, to which the adhesion of
the Argentine Republic was required, but which Republic
maintained the strictest reserve.

These facts, which were announced as great perform-
ances, but which have been duly explained in the statements

made by Chile on entering the contest with Bolivia and Peru respectively, conclusively show that the author and promoter of the war on the Pacific coast was Peru, whose Punic faith is well known to the governments and financiers of the entire world.

Chile entered the war alone, without assistance from any one, presenting a bold front to the malice of her neighbors, and to the sentiment which was everywhere created against her; thus it was that she advanced, upon the wings of victory, as far as Arica. She there consented to a Peace Conference, and frankly and almost imprudently proposed her terms. One of these was the cession of the coast, from the northern boundary of our territory as far as the Quebrada de Camarones (Shrimp Ravine).

The reasons which my government had, and has, for requiring that cession from its vanquished enemies as a partial compensation for the vast expenditures which it has been obliged to incur, in consequence of the war, are many, and their character is political, social, and economical. They are demanded by a regard for public order and for the peace of the continent, and are of paramount importance. My government will fully state those reasons, to which I have had the honor verbally to refer in my interview with Your Excellency, and this will render it unnecessary for me to perform that task.

As no peace was concluded at that time, Chile saw that Peru remained armed, and, as is said, stronger than before. The Peruvians repeated everywhere, and especially in the United States, that Chile was weakened, whereas her adversary had concentrated all her elements of strength in an army which was relatively immense and invincible.

It is, therefore, an error, and the error may be regarded as a malicious one, to say that Chile had it in her power to terminate the war at Arica, even though her terms of peace were not accepted. The most ordinary intelligence is able to understand that when we reached that place we had not gone more than one-half the distance which our duty imperatively required that we should go. We were obliged to go, and we did go, to Lima. Victory again crowned our efforts.

The Peruvian leaders Pierola, Montero, and the rest, fled to the interior.

We thought, as we had good reason to think, that the conquered country was exhausted, and we expected that the fugitives would come to make proposals of peace. As, however, such a thing could not be done instantaneously, we waited as long a time as was required by the circumstances. Meantime, we could not leave the great Peruvian zone (which included the entire coast, and which was controlled by our arms) a prey to anarchy. We did what our rights, our duty, and the dictates of humanity required us to do. Your Excellency will observe that I pass in silence over the incidents of the war, which have subjected us to so much obloquy, as is always the case in war, and to which even the United States were subjected in their contest with Mexico, and again during the war for secession; for, if I were to busy myself with these incidents, I should be obliged to enter into extended developments, which now belong to that history which is already written, and which has done us ample justice.

We had to organize the public service, and we did so with a lenity which I do not hesitate to characterize as highly reprehensible. Our action was at the outset exceedingly incomplete, and still is so, because, without going any further, the municipal administration and the postal service are still in the hands of the Peruvians. It was not possible, humanly speaking, for us to permit the misgovernment, the anarchy and the continuation of the nefarious Peruvian *regime* to exist before our eyes. We needed, moreover, to derive some resources from the conquered country (as has been done in all wars) in order to defray the expenses which we had been compelled to incur.

We fulfilled our mission in the best way possible, and in such a manner that, I firmly believe, no other nation could have fulfilled it better. We exposed the lives of our soldiers to all the hardships of a partisan warfare, which the Peruvians began to wage on every hand. Humanity required us to make those sacrifices, and we made them. If we had abandoned Peru under those circumstances, neither Lima nor Callao would now be standing, as attested by the fatal night of January 15th.

The fugitive leaders sought refuge among the mountains, and there they began to collect men and to proclaim war to the knife against the Chilians. Instead of being willing to treat on the basis of the Arica Conference, they declared again and again that the national territory should not be dismembered. This was not patriotism, for there is not a spark of that feeling in Peru; it was merely a pretext to keep on devastating the country, and to secure a foothold in its internal politics. They said that if any territory was ceded, civil war would be proclaimed in the country, whereas the endemic revolutions of Peru have never required causes, and with cessions of territory or without them, anarchy was a necessary consequence of the errors and crimes expiated at Tacna, Arica, San Juan, and Miraflores.

It was therefore totally impossible to treat with anybody. The Peruvian leaders not only had no power and prestige in the country, but they had no disposition to make peace.

I ask, what could be done? Were we to abandon the country and concentrate our forces in the South again? There was not a single reason, either political or military, to recommend such a measure, but on the contrary, there were the strongest reasons to adopt the opposite course. Chile, if she had abandoned her work and retired to the South, would have been ruined, and would have opened the door to a struggle whose duration it would have been impossible to foresee.

The Peruvian leaders were never without agents in the United States, in Europe, and in Panama; through these agents they procured arms and other elements of destruction. If they had been suffered to carry on their work, they would have collected their armies with perfect impunity, and would have rendered it necessary for us to undertake another expedition to Lima, besides which they would have constantly harrassed us in the South.

The duties of the strictest humanity, moreover, rendered it obligatory upon us to maintain public order on the Peruvian coast. This is so true that those very philanthropists who now undertake to bolster up the cause of Peru, say that it would be an act of barbarism on our part to evacuate Lima, inasmuch as that city would then fall into the hands of the freebooters, who are but a short distance from it.

To this must be added that men of standing daily called upon the Chilian General and the Minister of War, requesting them to adopt measures calculated to bring about the annexation of Peru to Chile, because they considered that to be the only salvation of the first named country. At the same time articles appeared, written by Peruvians, in various newspapers, particularly in the Panama *Star*, under the significant heading of "Annexation or Anarchy."

Chile had to do what she did, for it was impossible for her to do otherwise. She allowed public sentiment time to assert itself, she offered every imaginable opportunity for the resumption of peaceful pursuits, she established newspapers to advocate the most conciliatory views, and she then expected a reaction from the feelings of hatred then prevalent to take place, and reason to assert her sway.

All temporizing was useless, and was regarded as weakness. The guerrilla bands increased, the leaders collected larger forces, and the state of war continued in full blast.

The Peruvians have sought to excite universal execration against the Chilians, saying that they committed acts of vandalism during their occupation of Lima, and they point to the seizure of several chemical laboratories and cabinets containing natural curiosities; also of a library. The articles contained therein were defective and deteriorated, and their value was exceedingly small. If sold at public auction they would not have brought fifty thousand dollars. They are now in places where whatever of value they do possess will serve to promote the diffusion of knowledge. In the meantime, while these acts were going on, which are deserving of no attention whatever, Chile preserved the peace of Peru, rendered her cities safe by establishing a thorough system of police, punished plunderers, and spent very nearly a million of dollars every month.

It has likewise been said that the Chilians derived great profit from the productions of the Peruvian coast, particularly from those of Tarapaca. In the statements dictated by interest which have been published on this subject, there are glaring exaggerations, and a great want of candor. It is true that Chile has, of late, derived some benefit whereby it has been enable partly to defray the expenses of the occupation, but that benefit is far below what is claimed. When the statements of the Chilian Minister of War are cited, it is not considered that he was speaking of gross receipts, and those too in depreciated money; that those receipts were almost entirely expended in defraying the cost of the civil and military administration of the occupied territory, and that the said receipts have been extraordinary, and due in great part to the preparation of saltpetre which the government carried on at the outset, on its own account, when almost all the establishments were doing nothing.

Even admitting, however, that Chile has hitherto reaped some advantage, this is perfectly natural, just, and a rigorous consequence of the laws of war, and all that she has gained is no appreciable part of the enormous debt which Peru owes her.

It is proper to remark here that when two nations are fighting as allies, they are under obligations as jointly responsible debtors, to pay for the damage done by them.

During the period of forced expectation, while the Chilians were giving time for the vital forces of the country to revive, the anaemic government of Garcia Calderon was formed. Chile did not create that government, as has been asserted, but merely tolerated it and lent it some support, that it might acquire a certain degree of strength, and appear qualified in the eyes of the world to conclude a treaty of peace.

It is an inexcusable error to speak, at the present day, of legitimate governments in Peru, and Mr. Hurlbut, at Lima, has committed that error in calling the government of Garcia Calderon legitimate and almost constitutional, and that of Pierola a revolutionary government. Both are equally spurious, irregular and unconstitutional, as is apparent to the entire world. Chile has never entertained any other opinion; she has, however, given such aid as was proper without compromising her neutrality in the internal politics of the country to Garcia Calderon, that his government might become invested with the character of a *de facto* government. Under these circumstances it was recognized by the Government of the United States, which was actuated by a desire to terminate the bloody drama of the Pacific. This circumstance, however, in itself, does not make an irregular and abnormal government a legal and constitutional one; still less can it lay claim to such a character when, in the interior of the country, there are leaders who are likewise called governments, and who have more power and independence than that which has received recognition.

Garcia Calderon knowingly accepted the mission of peace which he was obliged to fulfil, and seemed perfectly resigned to it. The Chilians expected, and with good reason, too, that when that gentleman should once have the support of a Congress, whether constitutional or not, and whether with or without a legal existence, he would feel that he had force sufficient to conclude and sign the required peace.

While these things were going on months passed, which the friends of Peru seek to charge to the account of the illegal occupation by Chile, not remembering that they themselves have said that we were the custodians of the Palladium of peace on the Peruvian Coast.

Garcia Calderon held a number of private conferences with the diplomatic agent of Chile, and although he said that, for his part, he was ready to sign a treaty of peace based upon a cession of territory, he never dared to do so, because the people were opposed to that condition. He resorted to many shifts for the purpose of gaining time; and in the mean time it was publicly said that Mr. Christiancy, the American Minister, was encouraging him in his resistance. A considerable time passed thus, until at last the

Chilian agent was obliged to go to Chile, in order to inform his government, verbally, of what was going on;

While he was absent, Garcia Calderon fell into the most lamentable discredit, and was guilty of sundry acts of the most glaring bad faith towards Chile. The Chilian General had furnished him with six hundred Remington rifles, to enable him to arm a home guard, on the express condition that he was not to have more than those six hundred pieces, which were to be of the aforesaid manufacture. The troops at Magdalena, however (at which place the provisional President was allowed to exercise his jurisdiction), began to desert with their arms, the President offering not the slightest opposition, and adopting no measures to prevent the desertion. The said troops were, for the most part, prisoners of war, who had been released on giving their parole of honor not to take up arms against Chile. The deserters all went to fill up the ranks of the guerilla leader Caceres. When General Lynch was obliged to take away the arms which he had lent, he found that instead of the six hundred Remington rifles, there were twelve hundred, which were, for the most part, of the Peabody manufacture, and that there were, besides, other arms, about one million two hundred thousand rounds of ammunition, and a small machine for manufacturing cartridges. This alone would have been more than sufficient reason for sending the President home. Yet, according to the logic of some persons, Chile cannot do what it is lawful for any man to do it in his own defence.

In addition to this, it was known that Garcia Calderon had fraudulently ordered notes to the amount of forty millions of *soles* (dollars) to be printed by the American Bank Note Company, and that he had drawn bills in favor of private parties, for the purpose of introducing that money into the country. It is not positively known whether any portion of those notes was introduced into Peru, but it is certain that the bills drawn by Garcia Calderon were found in the fiscal bureau of which the Chilian General subsequently took possession. The merchants, who were mainly foreigners, were greatly alarmed at that clandestine issue, and the paper became considerably depreciated in the market, to the detriment of everybody, especially the army of occupation.

This, however, was not all. Mr. Christiancy had been succeeded by Mr. Hurlbut, who, as soon as he set foot in Lima, declared himself to be a warm friend of Garcia Calderon, and gave ground for the rumors that the United States would protect the territorial integrity of Peru. These rumors daily gained consistency, and acquired the character of evidence, when Mr. Hurlbut allowed copies to be taken and published of the memorandum which he had written of a private conversation held by him with General Lynch on the 25th of September last, and he afterwards likewise permitted the publication of a letter addressed by him, on the 12th of the same month, to Garcia y Garcia, Pierola's ministerial factotum, in the former of which he gave it to be understood that the United States would not approve of the dismemberment of Peru by Chile, and in the latter, openly said that Garcia Calderon would never consent to a cession of territory.

No other course, therefore, remained for the Chilian General to take than to put an end to that spectre of a government, which had been conditionally tolerated, but never formally recognized by the Government of Chile, inasmuch as Garcia Calderon had assumed an attitude of open hostility towards us. To permit a continuance of that provisional state of things would have been profitless, and, in a word, a mere mockery, so far as Chile was concerned. While the Chilians were protecting Garcia Calderon with their bayonets, he was declaring that he would not treat on the basis proposed.

But there was something more, Garcia Calderon had asked his Congress, which was composed of his friends, to authorize him to treat for peace, but all, with one accord, made it a *sine qua non* that he should cede no territory, and that he should maintain the integrity of the soil of Peru, according to the constitution.

The provisional president had shown himself indifferent to the desertion of his troops. It became necessary to strike a still more telling blow. The Chilian General resolved to dispossess him of the bureaus which he had organized ; but, instead of doing so silently and unexpectedly, he notified him of his intention by letter. Garcia summoned his friends, and also, it is asserted, a high foreign functionary, and drafted a refusal to comply, basing his action on the false ground that he was not a belligerent, since Chile had recognized him as legitimate President of Peru. The general immediately replied, denying that assertion, and detailing all the circumstances upon which he based his view of the situation. Garcia rejoined very humbly, rectifying several assertions, in his way, and General Lynch answered by means of a mere note of politeness.

Possession of the bureaus was taken, and the Chilian General promulgated the decree of September 26th, in which he absolutely denied Garcia Calderon's right to exercise jurisdiction.

I assert that no General in chief or government would, under the same circumstances, have acted otherwise, even supposing Garcia Calderon to have been recognized by all the neutral powers of the world, instead of by the United States and Switzerland only.

I fully appreciate the motives which induced the American Government to recognize Garcia Calderon as President, and even if it had had no other, its desire to open a way to peace would have been sufficient to justify its course.

It may, however, be made a question whether Messrs. Christiancy and Hurlbut, by acting in the manner stated, in the various emergencies in which they have caused their action to be felt, have contributed to the promotion of that end, and have faithfully interpreted the instructions which they have received from their government.

If there were no ground for forming an opinion with regard to this matter, save the course pursued by the American Minister in Chile, the answer would not be attended with the slightest difficulty. And if we were, moreover, to seek for motives in the traditional policy of the United States, and the particularly friendly course pursued by them towards Chile, the negative solution of the problem would seem evident.

The question of a cession of territory interests no one but Chile and Peru, and if the latter has reasons, good or bad, for refusing such cession, the former has many reasons, of incontestable cogency, for requiring it. The sentimentality with which some persons would seek to defend Peru, while at the same time, they despise her, is not a serious element in an international controversy of this kind. The fear lest territorial dismemberment may become a doctrine in America is utterly chimerical, because the map of America, the conditions of possible wars, and all the other circumstances that may be invoked, present no analogy with the case now under consideration. When Peru, moreover, appropriated the provinces which belonged to Ecuador, and which she still unlawfully holds, there was no such display of sentimentality; and the reason is that in the one case the private ends of third parties are concerned, whereas, in the other, no speculators sought to derive advantage from the quarrels of Ecuador.

After hearing this plain statement of facts, without any comments, how can any one say, with the faintest show of reason, that Chile has too long treated Peru with undue harshness, and that she is responsible for the delay in the settlement of the difficulty? What other country in the world could have accelerated the time whose advent Chile desires more than any one else? The converse of this proposition is strictly true. It may, and ought to be said to Peru, "You have had ample time to make peace, you have been able calmly to reflect upon your situation, and to adopt the only course that is counseled by sound reason and by a true regard for the interests of your country."

How can any one take an opposite view, ignoring facts which are patent to the whole world, and holding Chile responsible for omissions and delays which are really to be ascribed to Peru alone, is something that I am wholly unable to comprehend.

It is true that Chile might, a few months since, have waged a war of extermiation in the interior of Peru, and also in the north and south; but then it would have been said that my countrymen were a nation of blood-thirsty wolves, without compassion even for their own soldiers, who have been with arms in their hands for nearly three years, and we should have been held up to the execration of mankind. I should be glad to be told how else it would have been possible to act, in order to avoid the criticisms now so freely indulged in against Chile.

But even supposing that Chile had exterminated the guerrilla bands led by Pierola, Solar, Caceres, Albarracin, Montero and a dozen others, would the condition of affairs be different from what it is? Would peace have been secured? How, and with whom?

The acquisition of a portion of territory is something that is not forbidden, and is not a punishable offense; and I cannot see why Chile should not be left at liberty to acquire that which she is entitled, on a hundred grounds to expect. The entire course which she has pursued of late, tends to that end alone, and she will continue in that course until she gains her object.

Nobody can doubt that the territory in question will be better governed by Chile than by Peru, and that both native and foreign citizens will enjoy greater security under the new flag than under the old. The only ones who can question this are those who have, or think they have, private interests at stake in the quarrel or in the present juncture.

The pronunciamento of Arequipa and Puno has not changed the aspect of affairs. Garcia Calderon's Government has not derived any strength from that, and even if it had gained anything, the problem, as regards Chile, would still remain the same.

The pronunciamento of those two cities was not due to any attachment which they felt for Garcia Calderon, but to causes which I may call heterogeneous and foreign to the objects had in view. Those causes were principally three, namely, hatred of Pierola's tyranny, together with the exhaustion of the resources of those districts, fear of the Chilian expedition, which was already announced, and the hope with which the Peruvians have been inspired, of intervention by a nation whose policy has hitherto favored intervention less than that of any other nation of the world, namely, the United States of America.

To this it is added by some that certain of the so-called principal men of Peru have asked that their country may be annexed to the United States, and Garcia Calderon is represented as the chief advocate of this project.

The self-styled Magdalena Congress, after its adjournment, privately reassembled for the purpose of offering the first Vice Presidency of the Republic to Montero, and it was said that it was going to offer the second Vice Presidency to the partisan leader Caceres. It will also be sought to give a character of legality to these political buffooneries, which are without example in history of any country.

But whatever may be the position that Garcia Calderon is destined to occupy, the problem will not be a whit nearer to solution. The Gordian knot will still be firmly tied. The alternative between a cession of territory and war will remain so long as the Peruvians have any hope of intervention from without, or so long as they are encouraged with financial schemes by foreign speculators.

It now seems to me that the proper time has arrived for referring to one scheme, which, according to public opinion, in which I do not in this case put the slightest faith, is one of the elements which are active in this matter of peace, and which has given rise to the excess of sentimentality to which I have repeatedly alluded. In mentioning the private interests concerned in this matter it has been my purpose to refer to the schemes of which I am about to speak, and particularly to the

PERUVIAN COMPANY.

We all have more or less knowledge of the various financial schemes concocted in the French market, almost always under the auspices of the banker Dreyfus, the object of which is to get control of the guano and saltpetre trade. I am familiar with their history, and I know the course that things took, and the vicissitudes through which they passed, until a special commercial and financial company was formed on the South American coast. The originator of those manœuvres was Pierola, who, as is well known, is a great friend of Dreyfus.

No fact is better known than that delegations came from France to the United States for the purpose of interesting the government of this country in the realization of plans which were said to be designed to promote peace and civilization in South America.

The French merchants declared that they would undertake to pay any war indemnity that Chile might require, and that they would make an arrangement with Peru for the extraction of guano and saltpetre.

Equally well known is the plan proposed by Dr. Cabrera, Minister of Bolivia, in the United States, which he submitted to the consideration of the Department of State in February last.

It appears that none of these schemes met with favor in mercantile circles in this country, and that they did not receive the support of persons who, by reason of their political position, could lend them influential aid.

There is, however, another scheme, beyond a doubt the wildest one of all, which is said to have gained some *prestige* in those circles, and which is now considered as a factor in the problem of peace on the Pacific coast. I have frequently heard this talked of, and have seen references to it in print, yet I am unable to put the slightest faith in such ideas, for in order to do so it would be necessary to have lost all confidence in the common sense and the honor of mankind.

Never was a plan conceived that revealed more profound ignorance of facts, more sordid ambition, greater boldness, greater abuse of public credulity, greater contempt for the fundamental principles of society, than that which appears in type under the title of "The Peruvian Company."

The plan of the company is as follows:

"We are the owners of certain claims which Messrs. Cochet and Landreau had, or said that they had, against Peru. We estimate the value of these claims at about twelve hundred millions of dollars. We will induce Peru, which has never recognized this debt, to recognize it now. When it is recognized, we will declare that we are entitled to take whatever we can find in the territory of Peru, provided that it seems to our advantage to do so—guano, saltpetre, mines, agricultural property, etc., no matter who may be the owners of these things, and whether they be Peruvians or foreigners. As to Chile, we will pay her an indemnity in money; but, if her demands appear very high, she shall be compelled to submit the amount to arbitration."

Frankly, sir, this is the first time that I have heard, in a civilized country, any one dare to assert the doctrine that a creditor, because he is a foreigner, has a right forcibly to seize upon all private property found in the nation which is his debtor, no matter by whom it may be owned. Writers on international law say that a creditor may, in certain cases, as a last resort, seize upon strictly national property; that is to say, property belonging to the State or Nation; that he may collect taxes, and in extreme cases levy new ones; but they never say that he may deprive individuals of their personal property. This is a thing which has never been seen in the history of modern nations, although other irregular acts have been contemplated, which Chile has never been willing to imitate. The Peruvian Company proceeds on the supposition that Chile entertains the same designs that it does itself; this, however, is an error which must be considered as an intentional one, because what Chile desires is to become mistress of the soil, leaving every owner of property in the quiet and undisturbed possession of what belongs to him. The plan proposed by the Peruvian Company is just the opposite of this, for it maintains that the guano, nitre, and the copper, silver, and gold mines of Peru are all to go toward paying its claim.

That company, with the view of exciting the greed and avarice of speculators, has carried its powers of invention so far as to state, in its prospectus, that saltpetre is of such a nature that it renews itself every three or four years, like the sporadic plants which are found in all parts of the world. Hardly would one of those mountebanks who gain a livelihood by fortune-telling, dare to make such assertions before a tribe of Indians. The other statements of the company are on a par with this.

It has not yet been precisely ascertained what is the origin of the formation of the *caliche* beds from which salt-petre is taken. Many hypotheses have been advanced in explanation thereof, and the last, which is very ingenious one, supposes that these strata are formed from sea-weed deposited in the geological basins at a very remote period.

I do not propose to examine how the Peruvian Company can claim to be the owner of these shares which once belonged to Cochet & Landreau. Neither do I propose to discuss the question whether (inasmuch as those shares originally belonged to French citizens) the United States can properly uphold a claim in view of the fact that they are now in the hands of Americans. The doctrine laid down in the conventions with Spain and France, which is the subject that occupies the attention of the mixed commissions now sitting in this capital, protests against such a principle.

If I were in the place of Peru, I think it would be very easy for me to show that the claims of Cochet & Landreau, which neither France nor the United States have ever been willing to defend, are evidently unjust, apart from their colossal exaggeration. It is not, however, now necessary for me to busy myself with these aspects of the question.

What strikes my attention is the fact that, whatever may be the action of Cochet & Landreau, or their successors, against Peru, it is an action which is merely *personal* or *ad rem*, and not *real, rei persecutoriæ* or *in re*. They may recover a debt from Peru, but not this or that thing.

To this must be added that the only considerable deposits of guano now existing in that territory, are those of Gua-nillos, Pabellon de Pica Bahia Independencia and Lobos Afuera, not one of which appears among the alleged discoveries of Cochet & Landreau. Some of those deposits, moreover, are so poor that the guano found in them cannot be considered as fit for commercial purposes. The latest analysis made of the guano of Lobos Afuera show only two and a-half per cent. of azote, and from 12 to 13 per cent. of soluble and unsoluble phosphates, and guano containing less than 5 per cent. of azote has never been brought to the United States, while much of that brought has contained 7 per cent. of this element.

With regard to the quantity of guano found in the territory of Peru, it is relatively small and can excite the greed of no speculator.

I think it is undoubted that Peru published, in London, an immense list of new deposits, in order to make her last loan a success; it was soon found, however, that this was a mere trick, and that almost every one of the pretended deposits was utterly worthless, owing to their smallness, their inferior quality, the difficulty of extracting the guano from them, and the mixture of that article with earth, sand and stones, in addition to which many of them had no existence save in the imagination of the promoters of the loan. As to the Chincha Islands, everybody knows that they have been entirely exhausted for more than fifteen years.

To all the foregoing must be added the fact that the holders of Peruvian bonds in Europe, particularly in England, consider themselves as having a claim to the guano. Chile, without admitting the legality of this claim, has adopted a conciliatory course, allowing the guano at Tarapaca to be exported and consigned to Messrs. Gibbs & Sons, of London, on condition of receiving a royalty of one pound ten shillings sterling per ton, and with the proviso that the remainder of the proceeds shall go towards paying the bondholders.

The Peruvian Company, building castles in the air, would violently re-act against those facts and those rights, in order to get possession of the guano.

As to the saltpetre, the question is still more complex. Chile does not care whether the saltpetre works belong to Englishmen, Frenchmen, Germans, Italians or Americans. Chile is not the owner of those establishments, nor has she any wish to be. Her part, as a State, is simply to collect an export duty, which may vary in amount, and even become reduced to nothing, according to times and circumstances. Chile's chief concern is to protect the persons and property of her own citizens, situated in the saltpetre producing districts. The interests of foreigners, belonging to all neutral nations are protected at the same time.

The Peruvian Company proposes to abolish all rights in private property, in order to secure a monopoly of saltpetre. Nothing could be a greater blunder, in whatever aspect it be considered. But confining myself simply to a mercantile point of view, it will be sufficient for me to inform your Excellency that on the coast which formerly belonged to Bolivia, there are immense deposits of saltpetre, principally in the district called Toco, and on the lands owned by the Chilian corporation known as the " Antofogasta Saltpetre and Railway Company," also, on the coast which has never ceased to be the undisputed· property of Chile, there is an immense district containing deposits of that article of a very superior quality.

In order that the saltpetre trade may not bring disaster upon the individuals engaged in it, and upon the State, it must be governed by one code of laws and be subject to but one control. Otherwise competition will benefit the consumers, but will ruin the producers. Chile has not yet solved the problem of how this danger, which is patent to all, is to be avoided, but she is now attempting to do so.

The very trifling profit which Chile has thus far derived from the extraction of saltpetre at Tarapaca has been abnormal, and has been due to the fact that the greater part of the establishments were doing little or nothing, which rendered it possible to levy heavy taxes upon producers. But when competition shall throw a greater quantity upon the market than is needed, the price will fall, and the State will not be able to collect even a tenth part of what it has hitherto collected; if it do so, it will inevitably ruin private individuals engaged in the production of this article.

The Peruvian Company does not appear to have the most remote idea of how these problems are to be solved.

The average price of an English quintal of saltpetre has not, for ten years past, exceeded thirteen shillings, although it has brought a higher price during short periods, and under exceptional circumstances. For the chimerical plans of the Peruvian Company to have any foundation, it would be necessary that the consumption of saltpetre in the world should be *unlimited*, and that its average price should not be less than *twenty* shillings per quintal.

Everybody knows that there is a vast number of manufactories of artificial fertilizers both in Europe and America, and that very successful experiments are now being made with a view to extracting azote or nitrogen from the air and condensing it by chemical process. All these fertilizers are competitors with guano and saltpetre, and will render it impossible for them to rise above a reasonable figure or one proportioned to their commercial value.

The Peruvian Company affects to regard as a crime against civilization the attempt made by Chile to secure a small portion of territory as a partial compensation for the great sacrifice which she has been called upon to make. And how should the plan be regarded which that company says it is seeking to carry out? It is a matter of perfect indifference to it whether Chile takes a portion of the Bolivian coast or not; what it considers as an iniquity is that any portion of the Peruvian coast should be taken. Whence arises this difference of principles?

This scheme, which it is sought to represent to the people of the United States in the colors of the diamond, the sapphire, the emerald and other gems described in the Arabian Nights, is nothing but a piece of madness, which would compromise the policy of the United States in the most wretched kind of Quixotism. The fatal consequences of encouraging such a scheme would be felt not only now, but still more in years to come, and South America, far from deriving any benefit from the salutary influence of the United States, would appeal to that fundamental principle which forms the basis of the policy of this great nation.

CONCLUSION.

It is a perfectly logical deduction, from all the foregoing, that there will be no peace on the Pacific Coast so long as Peru continues to suffer herself to be deluded with the hope that her financial schemes, supported by this or that government, are destined to be realized, or that the intervention, more or less direct, of the United States is to come to her aid when she shall conclude a treaty of peace with Chile.

What interest of a universal, or international, or even of an American continental character, is to be subserved by promoting the continuance of this state of things, when it is evident that it will be necessary, at last, to see a war still more disastrous than that which has just drenched the Pacific Coast in blood, or to allow Chile the liberty of action which of right belongs to her, and which has been enjoyed by all nations which have been similarly situated? I am unable to see how any legitimate interest can be promoted by keeping alive those illusions of Peru; and I do not doubt that your liberal and enlightened views will lead you, Mr. Secretary of State, to share this opinion.

To characterize the course pursued by Chile as an abuse of force is an evident antinomy and a paradox. It would be necessary to characterize every military victory in the same way. The conqueror has a perfect right to dictate terms of peace, especially when he has conquered without the assistance of anybody, and has triumhped over the indirect opposition which has been systematically organized against him.

After the conferences held at Arica, Chile showed the world that her terms of peace had been remarkably just and moderate. When the proper time shall arrive for publishing the new bases which she will propose, and which are perfectly well known to Mr. Garcia Calderon and his circle she will do the same thing again, if she deems it necessary.

If Peru continues to give evidence of her absolute incapacity to defend her unjust cause by force of arms, and if she is also unwilling, as she has been hitherto, to make peace, the situation will be in all respects analogous to that depicted by Halleck, in his standard work entitled "International Law," (chap. 34) which has been very aptly quoted by one of the most accredited organs of public opinion in the United States:

"If the State to which the conquered territory belonged be so weakened by the war as to afford no reasonable hope of ever being able to recover its lost territory, but from pride or obstinacy it refuses to make any formal treaty of peace, although destitute of the requisite means of prolonging the contest, the conqueror is not obliged to continue the war to force the other party into a treaty. He may content himself with the conquest already made, and annex it or incorporate it with his own territory. His title will be considered complete from the time he proves his ability to maintain his sovereignty over his conquest, and manifests by some authoritative act, as of annexation or incorporation his intention to retain it as a part of his own territory. Both these requisites, *ability to maintain, and intention to retain*, are necessary to complete the conquest. . . If he incorporates the conquest with his former States, giving the people the rights, privileges and immunities of his own subjects, he does for them all that is due from a humane, and equitable conqueror to his vanquished foe."

WASHINGTON, *November* 21, 1881.

COMMUNICATIONS MADE BY THE CHILIAN MIN-
ISTER TO THE STATE DEPARTMENT.

November 10, 1881.

Sir :—I intend to proceed with the agreeable task of
informing you of the last authentic news from the Pacific
Coast, because they are generally published in a way calculated to mislead the public. Your Excellency has already
been made acquainted with the decree issued by the Chilian
General, P. Lynch, prohibiting Dr. Garcia Calderon from
exercising jurisdiction within the territory occupied by the
Chilian forces, though he may assume it without.

Indeed the Chilian Commander was unwarrantably mild
in allowing the so-called Provisional President to continue
his functions of a government. You will please allow me
to state again to your Excellency, that Chile never recognized
Garcia Calderon as the Provisional President, and that had
she made such a recognition it would have been annulled
when that gentleman made up his mind to reject the terms
of peace my government proposed to him.

In spite of the above named decree Garcia Calderon
went on assuming to himself the functions of President of
the Republic, but though pursuing a hostile attitude, the
Chilian General did not deem it necessary to take any measure against him ; and I assure your Excellency that the ground
for General Lynch's action was the recognition of Garcia Calderon, as Provisional President by the United States, purposely to lead the way to an arrangement of peace.

About that time Calderon's Secretary of State addressed
an official circular to the Diplomatic and Consular Corps,
stating that an acceptable settlement would soon be drawn
up, that is to say, one with no territorial compensation in
view.

This being an open and flagrant violation of the Chilian
Commander's decree, he was compelled to act promptly and

severely. He imprisoned the so-called Provisional President and his Secretary of State. This measure was executed most quietly. Mr. Garcia Calderon intimated that he wanted to hold a private interview with General Lynch, so he walked a long distance through the crowded parts of Lima, without the people showing any sympathy for him. The prisoners were treated in the best manner possible, transferred to the iron-clad "Almirante Cochrane," and dispatched to Chile.

Meanwhile the Peruvian General Montero being out of the reach of the Chilian forces has accepted the Vice Presidency of the Republic, and notwithstanding that such action was irregular, the Chilians keeping faith to their resolution of non-interference with the internal affairs of Peru, have opposed no resistance whatever to his assumptions.

A Peruvian Committee started from Lima to meet Montero and persuade him to proceed to Chimbote to propose terms of peace acceptable to both Republics. This incident suffices to prove that a settlement could have been arranged if the Peruvians had not deluded themselves with the vague phantom of foreign interference.

The ex-Dictator Pierola remains in Ayacucha with an army 1,700 strong. His Chief Secretary, Garcia y Garcia issued, under the date of 23d October, a circular addressed to the Chiefs and Governors of the Republic, bitterly criticizing Mr. Hurlbut's letter, with whose contents your Excellency is well acquainted.

The Chieftain Caceres, with an army stronger than Pierola's, is strongly intrenched in the neighborhood of Lima, apparently obeying the ex-Dictator, but really acting for himself.

Such is the plain story of the present condition of affairs in Peru.

It would not be unsuitable for your Excellency to become acquainted with a somewhat painful incident. Garcia Calderon intended to send to Arequipa one of his brothers as a commissioner, asking permission for him to be allowed to land at Mollendo, which is now a blockaded port. Not being permitted to do so, the latter obtained a passport from the Chilian Colonel, Valdivieso on the pretence of visiting a different place. After obtaining the passport the commissioner fraudulently altered it in order that he might reach Mollendo safely. But this was not all. Having obtained permission from general headquarters to reach a blockaded port, he did not avail himself of it, but seeing that the United States man-of-war Alaska was about to sail to Mollendo, he boarded that vessel, and after arriving there delivered money and correspondence to the rebels of Arequipa. Though I cannot vouch for it officially, I regard the story as sufficiently corroborated to warrant its publicity.

As for Bolivia, that country is practically out of the struggle, although General Camperon has an army 4,500 strong within a few days march of Tarapaca.

The Chilian forces, however, are prepared for any emergency, and would undoudtedly repulse any hostile attack of Camperon's.

It is logically inferred from the above that the enemies of Chile are again armed and as unwilling to make peace to-day as they were two years ago. They consider a settlement of peace as a virtual concession of their weakness, and from this mere matter of pride stubbornly refuse to yield.

Hence to ascribe the present state of affairs to Chile would be the grossest injustice and wholly inconsistent with the facts which I have stated, and a thousand others which could be advanced.

Accept, sir, etc.,

M. MARTINEZ.

To his Excellency, JAMES G. BLAINE,
Secretary of State.

———

WASHINGTON, November 26, 1881.

SIR:—Yielding to the purpose of communicating to the Department of State, the actual course of events that occur on the Pacific Coast, I shall briefly refer to the authentic information that I have had by the last mail.

Several of the military chiefs in Arequipa, availing themselves of the absence of Pierola and Colonel Solar, declared themselves in favor of the late provisional government of Garcia Calderon, giving the three following reasons for so doing:

1. That Pierola's tyranny was absolutely intolerable, that the country could not carry on the war with Chile, and that the United States had offered their intervention, in order to obtain an agreement of peace, that did not comprise territorial cession.

Certainly those patriots did not explain, how Peru could otherwise answer the claims of Chile.

Sometime afterwards, Rear-Admiral Montero, who had been for some months past, actively engaged on the Cajamarca mountains, accepted the irregular and unconstitutional offer of the Vice-Presidency of the Republic. In his letter of acceptance, dated October 23rd, 1881, he made declarations which are absolutely necessary that your Excellency should hear of, to know on what illusions the Peruvian leaders found their politics, and also to know the *role* which the American legation is made to assume in all those affairs.

The philosophy arising from the facts that I am about to state, is that while these illusions and hopes are being kept up, peace will be impossible.

Montero says : " The noble officiousness of the Government of the United States, manifested in the documents which have successively been published, even the *definite declaration* comprised in the letter written at the request of the *Notables de Lima,* by the Honorable Envoy, Extraordinary and Minister Plenipotentiary, from Washington—[a letter which nobody has seen] and which has completely changed the situation, and consequently its proper solution."

He adds, that he has officially communicated his resolution to the representative of the United States in a dispatch directed on the same day.

He finally states that " his noble wishes of increasing the elements to defend his country are greatly gratified !! " And concludes by assuring that " he redoubles his activity to multiply the necessary elements in order to be always ready for its support, till he sees the final issue of the diplomatic affairs with Chile!!"

If, as it is said, Garcia Calderon has been imprisoned because he insisted on disregarding the decree of the Chilian General within the limits occupied by the Chilian forces, it is probable that Montero will represent the provisional government, and I beg your Excellency to observe that this chief assures us that he has forces, and that he is desirous to have more to continue the armed resistance against Chile.

The protest of all these chiefs against a territorial cession, is established on the expectancy of American intervention, assured by Minister Hurlbut, to whom Montero has addressed himself as his immediate superior.

I have no doubt that your Excellency's keen judgment will lead you to the same conclusions.

All that is extraordinary and unexpected in the affairs of Peru will very often, I have no doubt, attract your Excellency's attention, and will lead you to conclude that Providence has not endowed that country with logic.

I have some reasons for believing that in some communications sent from Lima to the Department of State they insist on saying that the indemnity which Chile demands exceeds the limits of justice, and that the authorities in Lima have acted very cruelly towards the Peruvians.

This information is entirely erroneous.

As to the indemnity I will only say that those who think the claims of Chile are exaggerated, entitled as she is by the perfect right of the actual situation, are under a mistake, for these demands are moderate and equitable. They will doubtless be shown to be in conformity with the requirements of international law when the time comes to make them practicable. Those who think otherwise do it either out of dislike or want of knowledge in the matter, being incapable of judging of business matters that do not concern them.

As for the charge made that the Chilians have acted cruelly, we can state that if any virtue is to be attributed to the Chilians it is that of not being sanguinary. It is a fact, that during the space of eight years not more than three or four capital executions occur in Chile.

When the Chilian army occupied Lima the General-in-Chief invited the Peruvian tribunals to continue their functions, and they absolutely refused. It was necessary to establish a military tribunal governed under martial law in order to maintain public peace.

In a country greatly demoralized and given up to anarchy like Peru it was necessary to give examples of rigor, yet, nevertheless, there have been but few condemned to death, and those for acts of unheard-of cruelty.

Meanwhile society in Lima rests quietly under the auspices of peace and order guaranteed by the Chilians.

I shall continue to communicate to your Excellency any information, and in doing so this time, I renew my sentiments of highest consideration.

M. MARTINEZ.

To his Excellency, JAMES G. BLAINE,
        Secretary of State.

www.ingramcontent.com/pod-product-compliance
Lightning Source LLC
Chambersburg PA
CBHW030001030726
47499CB00008B/2840